IT'S ALL A MONSTROUS DECISION FOR—

THOMAS CARDIF—RHODAN'S rebellious son will destroy the galaxy, if need be in his fight against hellish retribution

ATLAN—Imperator Gonozal VIII is at an impasse but must step beyond!

Reginald Bell—The only way out of catastrophe is double-dealing against his dearest friend . . . Perry Rhodan!

Maj. Hunts Krefenbac—The *Ironduke's* First Officer stands on pride

Col. Jefe Claudrin—Epsalian commander of the *Ironduke*

Lts. Brazo Alkher & Stant Nolinov—The fugitives return in force!

Allan D. Mercant—The Chief of Solar Intelligence cuts a Gordian knot

Gen. Alter Toseff—The one active Arkonide general must cool his heels

Dr. Alonzo—Specialist in cytological research

Dr. Carl Riebsam—The *Ironduke's* mathematician

Maj. Albert Kullman—Commander of light cruiser *Zumbasi*, a fiddler with fate

Pedro Villaseluces—Kullman's unwilling copilot

Lt. Mark Dickson—Kullman's reluctant fire control officer

Maj. Burggraf—Commander of fast cruiser *Alcapulco*

Sonzomon—Springer skipper in very high dudgeon

Jeremy Mitchum—Guppy crewman; Brazilian

Buster Coleman—"Persuader" in the commando team

Sgt. Mulford & Lt. Yakinawo—members of the Space Infantry

Fleming—Communications man of the *Zumbasi*

Capt. Samuel Graybound—A rescuer

Dr. Gorsizia—A Physician aboard the *Ironduke*

Rall—A gyrocabbie

Leschtos—An Arkonide who must miss an audience with Atlan

Ufagar, Solaston & Petesch III—Legendary Arkonides of the past

THE ANTIS

Kutlos—The High Priest of Saos makes one mistake—his last.

Tasnor—His second-in-command is caught in the trap.

Hepna-Kaloot—Chooses the game of death.

Hanoor—The last survivor knows the meaning of ultimate freedom.

Egtoor & Agtlos—Witnesses of doom.

. . . and the spaceships *Ironduke, Zumbasi, Acapulco, Florida & F-32.*

ATLAN . . . CARDIF . . . AND MOUNTING HORROR

PERRY RHODAN: Peacelord of the Universe

Series and characters created and directed by Karl-Herbert Scheer and Walter Ernsting.

ACE BOOKS EDITION

Managing Editor: FORREST J ACKERMAN

WENDAYNE ACKERMAN
Translator-in-Chief
& Series Coordinator

CHARLES VOLPE
Art Director

PAT LOBRUTTO
Editor

Sig Wahrman
Stuart J. Byrne
Associate Translators

Perry Rhodan

107

THE EMPEROR
AND THE MONSTER

by William Voltz

ace books

A Division of Charter Communications Inc.
A GROSSET & DUNLAP COMPANY
1120 Avenue of the Americas
New York, New York 10036

> This Issue Dedicated To
> **HENRY J. KOSTKOS**
> Whose Entire Stf Output
> Consisted of 11 Short
> Stories & The Novel
> "Earth Rehabilitators,
> Consolidated" between
> 1933 and One Last Gasp
> in 1940. Author of "The
> Man Who Stopped the Earth",
> "We of the Sun" and . . . "The
> Emperor's Heart".

THIS WAY TO THE ACTION

Prolog

THOMAS CARDIF *the renegade has taken over Perry Rhodan's place as Administrator of the Solar Imperium and nobody suspects that an imposter is at the helm—not even Rhodan's closest friends or the mutants.*

When Cardif's actions differ strangely from those which would have normally been expected of Rhodan, an excuse for the Administrator's behavior is found in the fact that his mental health has suffered greatly as a result of his imprisonment by the Antis.

Knowing that no one has seen thru his disguise, Thomas Cardif triumphantly wields his power at will—even tho his actions may bring the races of the Milky Way to the brink of destruction.

However, the Usurper has failed to include one factor in his plans:

Another factor is Atlan, the Imperator of Arkon—because the situation becomes extremely critical for Perry Rhodan's impersonator when there is an encounter between THE EMPEROR & THE MONSTER . . .

1/ BEAST AT BAY

TREMBLING.

His hands were trembling. His facial muscles tensed and he unconsciously ran his fingers over his uniform as tho for comparison.

Altho Maj. Hunts Krefenbac, First Officer of the linear-drive warship *Ironduke*, had a reputation for being self-controlled, the present situation was something he had never been prepared for. Who could have told him he would ever see the Chief in such a condition as this?

As he glanced surreptitiously at the tall figure of the Terran he believed to be Perry Rhodan he experienced an instinctive sense of horror and alarm. Strangely, the Administrator's top uniform button was the most fascinating focal point, not only because it bore the highest rank emblem in the Solar Imperium but especially because it had been let out to the last fastener on his collar. In spite of this, Rhodan's jugular vein was prominently swollen due to the tightness of the largest uniform available on board.

Krefenbac couldn't take his eyes off the Chief's reddened face. It seemed to be broader and flatter than ever before. He wondered if the runaway process of cell division was actually going to continue like this without abatement. He heard someone urgently clear his throat as tho to warn him. It was Reginald Bell. But the warning came too late. The unsuspected imposter, Cardif-Rhodan, turned around with such a violent movement that the insignia button popped loose from his collar.

A dead silence pervaded the Control Central of the *Ironduke*.

The Chief's mouth had opened as if to speak but he failed to utter a sound. The button shield rolled in ever narrowing circles on the deck until it finally came to rest directly in front of Dr. Carl Riebsam, the chief mathematician. All eyes stared at the gleaming button as tho hypnotized.

In a momentary reaction of mortification, Cardif brought both hands to his throat and felt of the torn fastener. In a somewhat cracked voice he challenged Krefenbac. "You were about to say something, Major?"

There was a mixture of helplessness and sympathy in Krefenbac's expression. "Sir . . . " he began but groped cautiously for words.

Cardif suddenly drew himself up to his full height and the uniform stretched tightly over his body. It was no secret to the crew that in the past 3 days he had grown 3 cm and had also expanded his girth. It almost seemed as if the whole process were accelerating as they approached the planet Saos.

"Well, speak!" shouted Cardif, losing his composure. When he saw Riebsam bend down to pick up the button he pushed the mathematician out of the way. There was a nasty smile on his lips. "No, Doctor," he said scornfully, "not you!"

Krefenbac's face took on a slightly rosy hue. Reginald Bell stood with folded arms behind Cardif, whom he mistook for his best and closest friend.

Cardif glared threateningly at Krefenbac. "Well, Major, are you going to pick up that shield for your poor, sick superior?"

The color vanished from Krefenbac's face and he became deathly pale. He knew that Rhodan wanted to belittle him. The Administrator's and actions and mannerisms were incomprehensible to him. Krefenbac was a great respecter of discipline. He was an excellent soldier and officer.

"Sir," he said tonelessly, "please release me from this order. I'll bring you a replacement shield to your cabin."

It was obvious to everyone in the Control Central that the major had met him halfway. But everyone else knew that Krefenbac would go no further. Altho he was willing to lay down his pride he was not ready to bury it.

A fanatic gleam appeared in Cardif's eyes. He was able to interpret Krefenbac's attitude as well as anybody else. The major had backbone. Yet under the insidious effects of the cell activator Cardif-Rhodan could countenance no insubordination. He wanted *everyone* to obey him.

"Major," he half-whispered threateningly, "you will pick up the shield!"

Krefenbac tensed. His gaze met Cardif's squarely. Before he could say a word, everyone knew he was going to refuse the order. It was Bell who came to the rescue. He moved past Cardif, winked at Krefenbac and picked up the button himself. Cardif remained silent. Bell reflectively weighed the cause of the disturbance in his hand.

"If it means that much to you, Perry . . . "

He tried to give it to Cardif but the false Administrator turned on his heel and left the Control Central. Bell lowered his hand and the tension subsided. He had taken Cardif by surprise altho this solution had not been inopportune. After all, making such a test of authority with the major would not have had a good effect on the officer corps.

But such considerations were of secondary importance to Cardif now. For him there was one primary problem: how to bring his swiftly increasing size and weight to a halt and reverse the process? The only course that held any promise seemed to be an invasion of Saos. The priests of the Baalol cult had pushed him into this idea of procuring the cell activators from Wanderer. They must have known the frightful effect the device would have on him. Since they were not inclined to help him willingly he was going to have to force them to do it. Cardif was

11

no longer capable of thinking logically. The cell proliferation worked like a tumor, gradually interspersing immature brain matter among his normal nerve cells. He merely knew that he was backed up by the might of the Solar Fleet. And it did not occur to him anymore that he could be betrayed by the Antis.

He entered his cabin and made sure that the door was locked behind him. For awhile he stood there motionlessly in the room. Only the rise and fall of his chest gave a sign that he was alive. Then he started on a routine of activity that he followed every 12 hours.

He went to the opposite bulkhead where a vertical conduit casing served him as a measuring post. At the height of his head on the casing tube there were a number of variously colored markings, each accompanied by small figures representing dates. In total there were 5 such markings. Cardif picked up a ruler from a nearby table, then turned his back to the upright pipe. He placed the ruler on top of his head at right angles to the casing and then held it there while he turned and marked the spot with a colored penzel he had in his pocket. Taking the ruler away he saw that the mark was higher than the previous ones. With a trembling hand, he wrote in the date: *2 Sept 2103*.

Since the lastime he had stood here he had grown another half centimeter!

He suddenly struck the metal wall with his fist but the pain served to bring him back to his senses. From his pocket he produced a tape measure with which he carefully measured his waist. He then entered the figure in a notebook that lay on the table. Also here he noted an increase.

Cardif groaned softly to himself. He clutched at the place on his chest where the activator had half-buried itself in his flesh. The doctors had told him that it was no longer possible to remove it by surgery.

He knew it was useless to check his weight. It kept gradual pace with his increasing cell divisions. But he had another means of observing his condition which was much more conclusive. It was straightforward and brutal because there was no way he could be deceived by it. Rhodan's son hastily drew out from under his bed a mirror which was 1 meter wide and twice as long. This he set upright against the wall.

He saw himself standing there in the cabin with his arms at his sides and his hair all disheveled. Altho he did not actually appear to be ill there was no more of Perry Rhodan's muscular leanness to be seen. The oversized uniform was already too tight for him. With his fingers he felt of his body and noted that his flesh tone was no longer solid. Under pressure there was a certain sponginess to it.

Cardif stood there motionlessly as he regarded his reflection in the mirror. Inwardly torn by frustration, he felt that his burning hatred was ready to drive him out of his mind. He pointed to the image that was himself but which was supposed to represent another. The reflection simultaneously moved an arm to point to him.

"Hello, Rhodan!" he said in an almost garbled tone of voice. As tho listening for an answer he cocked his head to one side.

Was it himself or the image speaking now? "*Whoever* is Rhodan and holds his power firmly in his hands *must* be Rhodan! Do you understand?" A sneering mask of a face looked back at him. It had lost much of the once-chiseled features of Rhodan.

"The game goes on," said Cardif. "I will not give up so easily. Saos will fall!" He took a step closer to the mirror. Something stirred in his subconsciousness but failed to break thru. "Maybe I'll just keep on growing and getting heavier!" he half-giggled. "One of these days the *Ironduke* won't be able to hold me!'' The macabre vision of this seemed to amuse him. A confusion of thoughts shot thru his brain. He ripped open his uniform jacket and thumped his chest. ''Here is the fist of hell!'' he babbled in desperation. ''Its talons clutch my flesh and throb and pulse and give me no rest! Why can't you doctors help me?!''

No one answered him. He had always been alone. Somehow this thought reawakened his former pride. But only for a moment because as he started to straighten up, the uniform threatened to rip under the pressure of his increased size.

Was this the eternal life that he had promised himself with the falsely acquired activator?

He lay down on the bed to rest but found that he only tossed and turned. Should he order some more sleeping pills? A crazy idea began to creep into his mind. He imagined that while he was asleep Krefenbac would come in and he would be able to strangle him. Stupefied by the medicine he would not be able to defend himself in time.

He shook his head in desperation. He had to clear his mind. He must not forget his great goal. A large formation of the Solar Fleet was already in the Saos System. Involuntarily he happened to look again at the mirror. He got up and went over to it, strangely drawn to his reflection. He came so close to the glass that it became fogged by his breath. He wiped the patch of mistiness away with his sleeve in order to see better. Only centimeters away from the mirror's surface he stared into his own face.

And then he saw it!

He wanted to cry out or do anything but stand there staring, yet horror and panic momentarily paralyzed him. He finally groped behind him toward the table and grasped a heavy paperweight. He lifted it and hurled it against the glass. His face exploded into countless fragments. The splintered shards clattered to the floor, bringing him back to his senses. He staggered back to the bed and collapsed onto it.

It was his eyes which had shocked him so. Their gray coloration had appeared to fade as he looked at himself, to be replaced by a baleful yellowish tone. And Cardif knew what was in that look.

What had stared back at him was a beast of prey!

* * * *

Krefenbac took a long deep breath. His voice was full of heart-felt conviction when he thanked Bell for his intervention. "Sir, you saved me from a very unpleasant situation," he concluded.

Reginald Bell's expression remained grave. His freckled face was deeply etched with worry and it was plain to see how weighted down he was with his present burdens. On the one hand he sought to continue backing up his unfortunate friend and yet these men who surrounded him had to be shielded from his incomprehensible moods.

"The situation is unpleasant for *all* of us," he told the major. "We mustn't forget that the Chief is badly afflicted by his illness. Also the after-effects of his imprisonment on Okul are bothering him. I've discussed this thing quite thoroughly with Dr. Alonzo who is a specialist in cytology research. He says Perry is suffering from an explosive process of cell division."

"I wish I could help him," said Jefe Claudrin in his booming voice. "You know, when I think of what we're planning to do here I can't seem to shake off an uneasy feeling. Alkher and Nolinov reported that their escape was cleverly plotted out by the Antis. But they also infer that there were some slipups that the priests hadn't counted on."

"And from that we can conclude that the Antis wanted us to come here," said Bell. "There's some special reason for it. Their military setup on Saos isn't capable of standing up under a prolonged attack by our forces. They must be perfectly aware of that."

"But they have a flair for underhanded trickery," remarked Claudrin grimly. "We really ought to teach that bunch a lesson."

The colonel was a man of action. Under his command the *Ironduke* had become the most effective warship of the Solar Fleet. In addition to this was the fact that the 800-meter sphere was equipped with linear spacedrive. Within the Saos system at the present moment were more than 4000 Terran fighting units including a number of superbattleships. It was unthinkable that any alien vessel could slip thru this barrier of energy and steel without being detected. Nor could any spaceship take off from Saos and any attempt to land there would have been suicide. The Terran ships were deployed in a massive shell-like formation around the 2d planet of the sun known as 41-B-1847 ArqH. The small yellow star had no name other than the catalog designation. Of the 2 planets circling it the outermost was Saos. It fell under the jurisdiction of Atlan and the Greater Imperium since it was close to star cluster M-13, some 33,218 light-years from Earth.

By human standards Saos was an inhospitable world. The atmosphere was poor in oxygen content and consisted mostly of nitrogen and carbon-dioxide but the greatest problem was the planet's slow rate of rotation. A day and night period on Saos lasted 214 hours by Earth time, which brought with it the unpleasant effects that were largely typical of non-rotational worlds. Storms of hurricane magnitude raged in the transition zones between the day and night hemispheres and so all such regions were continually threatened by the violence of the natural conditions. Saos had not been able to develop any extensive areas of vegetation and had thus remained a desolate planet of deserts and wastelands.

It was not only from the descriptions of Alkher and Nolinov that Col. Claudrin knew what conditions faced him here, should the invasion actually take place. Like everyone else on board he was personally hoping that the secret of Rhodan's metamorphosis could be wrested from the Antis. Yet he did not know that this hope was a wolf in sheep's clothing. No one in the Fleet knew the real identity of the Administrator. Everybody was still inclined to follow the commands of the false Rhodan. Of course his physical alteration might have been countenanced by his friends with reasonable composure were it not for the change that was becoming evident in his character.

Since Claudrin was a logical thinker he was the first to correct his own statement. "What I mean is, we should make our move against the Baalol priests on a broader basis. If we don't know their plans we're facing a rather confused situation."

"Well, they're certainly not going to divulge them to us of their own accord," commented Dr. Riebsam with obvious sarcasm.

No one contradicted him. If any information were to be extracted from the Antis it would have to be done on Saos. But that seemed to be just what the enemy was waiting for. Bell, who in the absence of his presumed friend was trying to minimize his shortcomings, found himself in an unhappy situation. He had to prove to Rhodan that an attack against this Anti world would be senseless. But to produce this proof he had to land on Saos. The stocky First Deputy Administrator was beginning to suspect that the priests had set up a trap that the Solar Fleet could more or less stumble into if more precautions were

not taken. The hidden guarantee of the was Rhodan himself
—or the man who wore his mask.

* * * *

Kutlos' policy had been simple and successful. It consisted of
merely carrying out the instructions of the Baalol High Council
in every case. For this reason he had been advanced to the
officiating priest on Saos. If he ever felt in a contradictory mood
he would only express it to underlings. He believed that to gain
power one had to move among the mighty and know how to get
along with them. For him this principle had always paid off. To
other high priests Kutlos had always been known as a quiet and
rather inconspicuous type. But one day he had come to Saos in a
great long-ship and had taken over the office of the high priest
there. He had stepped tall and lean from the airlock and turned
his penetrating gaze to the industrial area.

The installations of the Antis had been located in an 8-km
basin surrounded by high and barren mountains. Being naturally
protected from sandstorms it was an ideal place for a Baalol
stronghold. The spaceport lay in the northern part of the
canyon-like enclosure and the nearby manufacturing center
stretched out about 2 km from there. There were also subterra-
nean installations which reached a depth of some 50 meters or
so. Here on Saos the Antis produced the projector-generators for
their individual defense screens.

In the center of the circular area a pyramid structure towered
to a height of 150 meters. Officially the Antis used it as their
temple. Around this imposing edifice were arranged a number
of long, low buildings in a square, and at the corners were 4
loftier structures crowned by metal domes. These marked the
location of the 4 major power plants.

Since the day of his arrival Kutlos had not made a single

change in the manufacturing operation unless it had been ordered by the High Council of Baalol. He submitted his reports at regular intervals and always avoided putting any pressure on his superiors or asking any inconvenient questions. Therefore, contrary to expectations, the High Council had become convinced that Kutlos was one of the most capable high priests in the entire sphere of influence of the Antis.

At this particular moment Kutlos was in the Saos observation center, which was located about halfway up inside the pyramid. Here the technical equipment had been installed for space surveillance. He was watching a slightly convex viewscreen which glittered with pinpoints of light that were evenly spaced across the entire field of vision. The trace blips appeared to be harmless but that was purely an illusion.

Every one of the glowing lightpoints represented a Terran ship. They formed a chain around Saos, preventing any Anti vessel from taking off or landing. Kutlos had been prepared for the arrival of a part of the Solar Fleet but he had not counted on its happening so fast. Transport ships loaded with high-precision machinery for the production of the individual defense screens still lay at the spaceport. Only the cylindrical ships of the Springers had been able to make a fast getaway in time. They

19

had completed their assignment of staging a sham attack against the stronghold.

Kutlos straightened up. The familiar humming of the air-conditioning recalled him to the present.

"Shall I shut down, Kutlos?" asked the operator, who was a young priest. He was referring to the viewscreen.

The high priest nodded silently. The countless tracking devices in the room were keeping every Terran ship under close surveillance. Each change of location was instantly registered by them. Special radiation sensors were carefully monitoring the energy output of every vessel so that the start of the invasion could be detected immediately.

To Kutlos' way of thinking the Terrans were holding off too long. By Earth reckoning the Fleet task force had been lying out there for 3 days already. The high priest had hoped that all the Antis could get away in the transport ships *before* the arrival of the Terrans. The swiftness with which the spherical warships had broken thru out of hyperspace had destroyed this part of the plan. Against their wishes the priests on Saos were forced to remain in the stronghold.

For the firstime Kutlos saw his strategy doomed to failure. In case of invasion the most vigorous counterdefense would eventually have to collapse. The high priest had no intention of giving up Saos without a fight but he knew it would end in destruction and defeat. Unobtrusively he ran a hand thru his hair. The ships surrounding the planet did not make him particularly nervous but he struggled with a sense of resignation when he realized that his path to power was to be blocked by the unexpected velocity of 4000 spaceships. Other than that he had no qualms: he felt that the manner in which he had conducted his life was justified.

A voice nearby intruded upon his deliberations. "When will they attack?"

He turned to look into the eyes of Tasnor, his deputy high priest. From the first day of meeting him, Kutlos had formed a definite opinion of Tasnor. The man was intelligent, considerably more intelligent than the high priest himself, but he would never rise to high honors within the hierarchy of the Baalol cult. Tasnor was guilty of 2 fatal errors: he talked too much and he talked with everybody. Moreover, he was always trying to mix in certain ideas of his own. Such a modus operandi was bound to hurt his career.

Kutlos regarded him in silence and Tasnor virtually froze in the cold glance of the high priest. To the latter it was immaterial what the younger servant of Baalol thought of him. Perhaps the man hated him but that did not alter the respect he gave him. In his association with the powerful and the mighty, Kutlos had learned how to gain such respect and to keep it.

"It's just that this waiting gets on a person's nerves," explained Tasnor.

Kutlos smiled in a way that reduced Tasnor suddenly to a nervous and inexperienced underling. The deputy high priest reddened; his eyes lowered and his hands fidgeted with his wide cape.

"I know," replied Kutlos, "but we should be grateful to the Terrans for this period of grace. It gives us time to carry out the second part of our plan."

Hepna-Kaloot turned in his seat. For an Anti he was a very small type and pudgy. "That sounds as if we still had a way out of this," he said. "It was never my intention to die a hero's death, Kutlos. What have you thought of that still gives you hope?"

Hepna-Kaloot was the only priest on Saos for whom Kutlos felt any sympathy. He tended to spare the little man from the treatment he accorded the others. Hepna-Kaloot had a way of transmitting to his surroundings the indifference he felt for all things. Even when he asked questions, as he did now, one felt that nothing could really disturb him. There was only one thing that could inspire the chubby little priest and that was the game called Paloot—an indulgence that was forbidden, of course.

However, Hepna-Kaloot was so familiar with the regulations that he could be suspected of getting around them from time to time. Occasionally on a quiet evening he would get carried away and start talking about playing Paloot. He had always represented himself as a mere onlooker but it was clear to his listeners that his role must have been otherwise and that he had actually been a participant.

So the most direct clue to Hepna-Kaloot's character was his gambling nature. But now they were all in a game together which was much more vital and for the firsttime the stakes were open on the table: this was a gamble for life itself. It was understandable that the little priest would have gladly pulled his stake from *this* game if the opportunity presented itself, so perhaps at the moment his words were a bit less indifferent than usual.

"I see no reason why we should not carry out the original plan," said Kutlos. "We shall adhere to the instructions of the High Council." Even before he had finished speaking he saw the gleam of resistance in Tasnor's eyes.

"When those orders came in from Baalol," the younger man reminded him, "we still didn't know that we would have no chance of getting away from Saos. The plans of the High Council were based on another premise."

Kutlos did not have to see the faces of the other Antis present to know that the majority of them shared Tasnor's view. And his second-in-command was quite aware of it. But this did not disturb Kutlos. This chattering gossiper would not prevent him from experiencing a final triumph.

"The only thing that has changed," said the high priest calmly, "is that we are still *here*."

Tasnor made the mistake of interpreting this as the beginning sign of weakness on Kutlos' part. He turned to the assembled Antis and raised his arms in a gesture of entreaty. "Kutlos is certainly right on that point!" he called out to them. "We are still here and all of our lives are in danger. 4000 ships are ready to attack the planet and they will give us no quarter. If we were to let this happen it would be a senseless sacrifice. So my suggestion is this: let us reveal to the Terrans who their supposed Rhodan really is. They will imprison him and return to Earth."

"That's a bad suggestion!" cut in the high priest sharply. "If the Terrans discover they have been taking orders from Cardif they will make every effort to locate the genuine Rhodan. And where, may I ask, would they be most likely to find such information but here on Saos?" Kutlos paused to let his question sink in. "So if they know about Rhodan's son they are still going to land here. In fact, having learned that we tricked them they may be more determined to take us than ever before." He waved a hand in rejection. "Let us not deceive ourselves! We all know what dangerous antagonists the Terrans can be. Why provoke them further? We still have Cardif in the palm of our hand. We must not throw our trump card away so easily. As long as Thomas Cardif still wears the mask of the First Administrator the ships of Earth are relatively harmless to us. The High Council of Baalol has informed us that they are much more concerned about another mighty one in this galaxy."

"Imperator Gonozal VIII," interjected Hepna-Kaloot. "The Arkon admiral of the Greater Imperium."

Kutlos knew that the rotund little priest was trying to tell him he would not join forces with Tasnor. Hepna-Kaloot always considered his decisions to be well founded and this the other

THE EMPEROR AND THE MONSTER

Antis were aware of. So Hepna-Kaloot's expression of loyalty was a great contribution to the high priest's prestige.

"That is correct," agreed Kutlos. "We know that Atlan is one of the few Arkonides who remained unaffected by the deterioration of his race, and since he took over from the robot Brain much has happened. Gonozal VIII acted with a strong hand and sought to shake the Imperium to a new state of wakefulness so that the deterioration process might come to a halt. And in this respect Perry Rhodan was a good ally. The 2 imperiums together constitute a mighty factor of power. The 2 leading men in both stellar empires came to be friends." Kutlos smiled sarcastically. "But now in the meantime our mutual friend Thomas Cardif has managed to change the situation decisively. Today there are political differences between Arkon and Terra. One can practically speak of a cold war that's going on. Our agents have learned that Cardif has withdrawn all Terran personnel from the Arkonide planets, where they were in strategic positions of the administration. Rhodan's son has probably offended the Imperator a number of times by now. Things have come to the point where Solar Fleet formations are maneuvering within the Greater Imperium itself."

Tasnor appeared to realize that this long-winded explanation was intended to win the priests over. "We know all that," he retorted stubbornly. "But it gets us nowhere."

The high priest did not allow himself to be distracted. As he continued to speak the volume of his voice hardly competed with the hum of the electronic equipment. What he said, however, was understood by everyone present. As ever before, Kutlos was careful not to interweave his personal thoughts into his exposition. He kept stressing the fact to his fellow Antis that he represented the will of Baalol. "Gonozal VIII has called for

24

general mobilization," he said finally. "This indicates that he considers a serious conflict to be an imminent possibility."

Kutlos slapped his hands together as tho to dispatch an annoying insect. He stood there, tall and lean, just as he had first appeared on Saos when he arrived on board the spaceship. He represented the High Council of Baalol which was the final and self-sufficient authority. It almost seemed as if an invisible strand reached down from the Anti leaders into Kutlos, imbuing him with their own totalitarian power. In effect, Kutlos was the long arm of Baalol.

"The High Council believes that we can help to agitate this conflict. Arkon and Terra are negatively disposed against our sect. So it's only logical that we should attempt to weaken both sides. To that end we can afford to sacrifice this base."

"And our lives along with it!" shouted Tasnor.

But he had already used this argument so many times that it failed now to have the desired effect. Kutlos had never doubted his own victory in this game of polemics and now he nodded to Hepna-Kaloot, who gave him a fathomless smile. By this Kutlos knew that Hepna-Kaloot was the only one whom he had not convinced. The wily little Anti was too adroit to admit it openly. The high priest was startled when he realized that Hepna-Kaloot was actually using his own strategy.

Kutlos concluded: "If Atlan and Cardif come to blows, we will have the last laugh," he explained. "This system is within the sphere of influence of the Greater Imperium. If the Solar Fleet attacks us it will be mixing into the internal affairs of Arkon—which is tantamount to opening the main invasion." He went over to the viewscreen again and turned it on. The tapestry of light points appeared as before. "The plan is good," he said. "And it will work."

With these few words, Kutlos had decided to destroy 4000 Terran ships—or better yet, to let them destroy themselves. If thousands of Arkon robotships were also destroyed in the process, nothing would please the Antis more.

* * * *

One of the blips of light on the Antis' viewscreen was the linear-drive warship *Ironduke*, which held a steady orbit around the planet.

Lt. Brazo Alkher's lanky figure moved along the corridor that led from the Control Central to the officers' quarters. Directly behind him was Lt. Stant Nolinov, whose stocky frame and blind stubble of hair contrasted sharply with Alkher's tall and bony physique.

The two officers had known each other ever since the first mission of the *Fantasy*. Together with Perry Rhodan they had survived the shipwreck and had been rescued by Capt. Samuel Graybound. A bond of friendship had developed between the two which was far more than the usual G.I. buddy relationship. From a military standpoint the two were a fantastically coordinated team. One Brazo Alkher at the fire control center of a spaceship was more deadly than 10 heavy cruisers.

If one were to question Alkher concerning his special abilities he would modestly reply: "I work the guns, that's all." But *how* he worked them was something else again.

Their imprisonment on Saos had drawn the two more closely together than ever. They knew that they had only one man to thank for their involuntary sojourn on the Anti planet—the man they all took to be Perry Rhodan. Cardif-Rhodan had ruthlessly abandoned them on the enemy's ship and on top of it had issued orders to open fire on the vessel.

"So *now* what does he want of us?" asked Nolinov. He had come to a stop. The mixed tone of suspicion and rejection in his voice was obvious.

Alkher shook his head regretfully. "You're talking about the Chief," he reminded his friend.

"Of course I am!" retorted Nolinov bitterly.

They had stopped in front of a cabin and now Alkher knocked on the door.

"Come in!"

Alkher opened the door and stepped into the small room. The floor was covered with the fragments of a shattered mirror. In some confusion, Alkher looked across at the bed where Perry Rhodan was lying.

The Administrator had taken off his uniform jacket and exchanged it for a bulky sweater. Over his eyes he wore a pair of dark goggles of a type used by technicians in the converter rooms. Alkher heard Nolinov come in behind him.

"You called us, sir?"

He could not make out Rhodan's eyes behind the opaque goggles. When the Administrator sat up, Alkher could not be sure whether he was looking at him or at Nolinov.

Unexpectedly, Rhodan seemed to be quite friendly. "You know that I consider you two to be my closest confidants," he told them.

"Yessir," answered the 2 lieutenants in unison.

Alkher felt rather than saw Nolinov's mystified glance. It was not evident to either of them why they should have arrived at such a special consideration.

"I selected you two to go to Wanderer with me," he reminded them. "Your special qualities have not escaped my notice."

Alkher felt his uneasiness increase. This whole approach was leading to something that was certainly not suitable for bolstering Rhodan's crumbling influence.

"We realize that, sir," said Alkher cautiously. He figured it was best for him to do the talking. Nolinov's impulsive nature might only get them into trouble.

As Rhodan stood up he stepped on one of the glass fragments and the grinding sound made Alkher shudder. Against the wall he saw the frame of what was left of the mirror. Apparently the Administrator had shattered it in a fit of rage.

"You were present during the undisciplined exhibition of Maj. Krefenbac," said Cardif-Rhodan. "You have witnessed how far an officer can go in his psychopathic arrogance."

Nolinov gasped audibly. Alkher nudged him with an elbow and hoped that Rhodan hadn't noticed it.

"We saw everything that happened," confirmed the lieutenant quietly.

"Maj. Krefenbac is the *Ironduke's* First Officer," said Rhodan, "but that's going to come to an end."

"Sir!" exclaimed Alkher, dismayed.

"I'm going to remove him from that responsible position," announced Rhodan. "It's just not suitable for that kind of a man to hold a position that is vital to the life of the ship. Major Krefenbac can't carry out a simple order—so what would he do in case of important decisions? I rather imagine that the major would lose his nerve in a space battle and would refuse to obey a command."

Alkher forced himself to remain calm. His thoughts were racing in new confusion. He regretted that Bell was not present. Rhodan's closest friend was still the only one who had any influence over this sick man.

Nolinov could not suppress a comment: "Sir, I regard Maj. Krefenbac as a capable man and as my superior officer."

Rhodan nodded. He had sat down on the bed again and his hands began to dig into the covers repeatedly—like claws. "That only proves that you don't have an eye for such men, lieutenant," he said. "It's important to study the men around you. You practically have to dissect their character, Nolinov. If you put them in a carefully planned psychological situation—as I did—then you will find sometimes that a villainous disposition can be lurking under a very polished façade."

"Yessir," replied Nolinov but his tone was cool and aloof.

Suddenly Alkher felt that Rhodan's eyes were fixed upon him behind the dark goggle lenses. He strove to meet his unseen gaze with firmness.

"Lt. Alkher, you appear to me to be good officer material," Rhodan informed him.

"I do my best, sir," said Alkher, and he tried to make his voice sound friendlier than he was feeling at the moment.

Rhodan nodded in satisfaction. "Lieutenant, I am going to appoint you First Officer of the *Ironduke*."

For a moment Alkher was too perplexed to think of an answer. The problems that loomed up behind this fatal offer seemed to him to be insurmountable. He blinked in his confusion.

Rhodan laughed hoarsely. "That probably comes as a surprise to you, Alkher, doesn't it?"

"That would be no exaggeration, sir," the lieutenant managed to say.

Rhodan got up and walked toward him over the cracking and crunching fragments of glass. Alkher involuntarily took a step back but Rhodan clapped him on the shoulder.

"You'll be able to handle it alright," he told him with a cordiality that seemed to be overdone.

It made Alkher wince. Nolinov seemed to have stiffened into

a post. Brazo glanced toward him helplessly then stared at Rhodan again. "Sir, I am grateful for your confidence in me," he stammered.

Rhodan's hand weighed heavily on his shoulder but Alkher didn't dare move. He suddenly remembered the firstime he had met Rhodan. He had mistaken him for a mechanic and had treated him accordingly. But the Rhodan he remembered was a different man from the one who stood before him now.

"You and Nolinov know that stronghold on Saos better than anyone," said Rhodan. "You are both capable of leading the attack against the Antis. With Krefenbac eliminated, nothing more can go wrong. I shall relay my orders thru you to the fighting units."

"Sir, I . . . " Alkher struggled to find words.

Rhodan's voice became sharp. "Perhaps you have an objection, Lieutenant?"

Alkher swallowed hard. His brown eyes acquired a feverish intensity. It was not the man himself who disturbed him so much—but his deeds, his history, his legend. With a courage born of desperation he finally blurted out: "Sir, I have to decline your offer—I'm very sorry, sir!"

"What?!" shouted Rhodan. "Are you insane, Lieutenant? I offer you the greatest chance of your life and you dare to refuse it?"

Brazo Alkher could only stare in wide-eyed consternation at the raving Administrator. He felt the color draining from his face and there was sweat in the palms of his hands. He fought against a tendency to tremble in his agitation. Nolinov stood tight-lipped and silent nearby.

"Are you working in collusion with this useless Krefenbac?" Rhodan continued to rave. "I will see to it that my commands are obeyed!"

"Every one of your commands is obeyed, sir," Alkher half-whispered. "However, the regulations permit me to think about a promotion or to decline it if I do not feel qualified to handle the new assignment."

"Out!" shouted Rhodan. "Get out!"

Alkher and Nolinov saluted stiffly and made a hasty exit from the cabin. It was only when they were at a safe distance that Nolinov finally expressed himself with a note of relief.

"I thought for awhile there you were going to accept the promotion."

Alkher was breathing heavily from his ordeal and a slow burn of anger brought the color back to his face in a hurry. "He almost had me fooled—until he brought up that button scene with Krefenbac. He's flipped!"

"Better watch that, buddy," said Nolinov, chiding him sarcastically. "You're *talking* about the Chief!"

Alkher was either thinking too intently to catch the innuendo or he preferred to ignore it. "I wish there were some way I could help him," he said. "It's obvious his rockoff actions are tied to this creepy sickness of his. Did you notice the oversize sweater he's wearing?"

"The biggest uniform in the Fleet won't fit him anymore, Brazo. But what's with those welder goggles? He must have borrowed them from one of the technicians."

A nameless fear gripped Alkher as he thought about this. "It's plain that he's trying to hide something."

"Maybe he thinks the alterations in his face would be too much of a shock for us."

Alkher sounded depressed. "Do you think he will die?"

"The doctors won't say this growth is malignant. It all depends on how his organs and brain will react to the unnatural increase of his cells." Nolinov waved his hands helplessly. "If

31

the medicos don't find a way to stop it there's going to be a real crisis sooner or later.''

"Yes, but *when?*''

As they entered the Command Central together, Nolinov muttered softly: "Who knows?''

The mood on board the *Ironduke* was depressed. No cheerful words rang out. The officers only looked silently at the 2 lieutenants.

"How is he, Brazo?'' asked Bell.

"He's very bitter, sir,'' reported Alkher. "He's planning to relieve Maj. Krefenbac of his duties. He offered to promote me to his position.''

"You hear that, Major?'' Bell called over his shoulder.

"Yessir,'' was Hunts Krefenbac's toneless answer. White-faced but self-controlled, the major had gotten up and walked over near Bell. In spite of his dejection he seemed to have more pride than ever. "I'll give you my bars, Lieutenant,'' he said to Alkher.

"No sir—no need for that. I turned down the offer. When I started to remind him of my rights under the service regulations, he practically threw us out of his cabin.''

Col. Claudrin's voice thundered at them. "You're still First Officer, Hunts. Either Rhodan has to remove you personally from your commission or he has to give me an order to that effect.''

"So I wait until it's official?'' asked Krefenbac bitterly.

"I'll go talk to him,'' announced Reginald Bell.

No one contradicted him. If there was anyone now who might talk some sense into Perry Rhodan it had to be Bell. He was the Administrator's closest friend. He had known him the longest.

"He's wearing a sweater now, sir,'' said Nolinov. "And a pair of welding goggles.''

Bell merely nodded to the men in silence and left the Control Central. He did not have much hope for the success of his mission. In recent days he had withdrawn inwardly from Rhodan. The ties of a true friendship, reaching across so many years, now seemed to have been torn asunder. Bell realized that his opposition to Rhodan's senseless orders was growing. The aftereffects of the shock treatment Rhodan had received on Okul were not subsiding at all.

When he came to Rhodan's cabin he figured it would be better to knock altho in other days such formality hadn't ever been necessary. In response he heard an angry voice yelling at him from inside. "Alkher, I told you to get out of my sight!"

Bell opened the door and stepped into the room. Rhodan was lying on the bed, just as the 2 lieutenants had described him. He raised up swiftly and scowled.

"It's only me," Bell told him simply.

Rhodan sank back and folded his arms behind his head. Apparently it would be only a matter of time before the bed would be too small for him. "What do you want?" he asked in an unfriendly tone.

"Just thought maybe you could use a little company," Bell explained calmly. "I'm not needed in the Control Central." He sat down on the end of Rhodan's bunk, noting that the other obviously regarded this with resentment. He decided it was best to ignore his friend's antipathy and his unpleasant mood. "Well, I see you're wearing shades, Perry," he said pleasantly. "Has something happened to your eyes?"

"Those miserable babblers!" shouted Rhodan, referring to Alkher and Nolinov. "Right away they had to go tell everybody!"

Bell watched him calmly. What was there left of Perry's famous self-composure? What had happened to the legendary cool and calculating objectivity that had always distinguished him as Administrator?

"Do you want me to send for Dr. Gorsizia?"

Rhodan laughed bitterly. His lips curled in derision. "What good can Gorsizia do me when none of the specialists of Terra can help me?" He tugged at his shapeless sweater. "Even my uniform jacket's too small!" He suddenly sat up and lunged at Bell, grasping him by his collar with both hands and bringing his face very close to him. Behind the dark lenses Bell thought he could make out the vague outlines of his eyes. Rhodan's hot breath was on his cheeks. "Look at me!" he demanded hoarsely. "Go ahead! Have a good look! I'm slowly becoming something inhuman—I'm turning into a bloated monstrosity!"

Bell pleaded with him. "Perry, for God's sake get hold of yourself! Now calm down!"

"Calm down!" he blurted. In his panting desperation he was anything but the Administrator now. "What do you know about the torture I'm going thru? Should I show you, Bell?" With a lightning movement he tore off the goggles and threw them aside.

Unable to speak, Bell looked into his friend's eyes. A yellowish fire of hate, despair, anger and fear was concentrated there. Bell suddenly recalled where he had been confronted by such a baleful glare before: as a youngster when he had visited the zoo and looked thru bars at a captive beast of prey.

"Their color has changed!" shouted Rhodan.

In spite of his iron nerves, Bell had to lower his eyes before the other's gaze.

"The Antis!" yelled Rhodan. "They're the guilty ones! And for that Saos must fall!"

At this moment the only thing Thomas Cardif had in common with his father was the name and the title he had appropriated.

More and more his own characteristics were overriding the positive hereditary factors of the genuine Rhodan. Cardif had become a hate-filled fanatic consumed by his own desire for revenge.

Deeply shaken, Bell got to his feet. His shoulders slumped visibly as he went to the door.

"Bell!" came a cry of consternation behind him.

He did not turn around because those wolfish eyes had burned themselves into his mind like points of inextinguishable flame. He only came silently to a stop.

"You have to stick with me, Bell!" pleaded Cardif-Rhodan in a half-croaking voice.

All Bell could manage at the moment was a mute nod of his head. Just that cost him more self-control than he had ever exerted in his life. The man on the bed was a stranger to him. There was no inner bond between them anymore. With uprooted emotions, Bell left the cabin. He had completely forgotten his own concerns.

When he returned to the Control Central, the only one to ask a question was Col. Claudrin. "What did the Chief say?"

When Bell looked at the Epsalian commander the latter's expectant expression faded.

"He took off his goggles," said Bell, almost inaudibly.

This was at exactly 18:45 hours, Standard Time. After that, no one asked anything more about Rhodan. A still deeper silence pervaded the Control Central. Everyone was waiting for Rhodan to appear. The arrival of the Administrator would unquestionably signal the start of the Saos invasion.

Undisturbed by all this, the *Ironduke* continued in its fixed orbit around the world of the Antis. Within its giant hull was a man whose sanity was being clouded more and more by his frightening cell growth. This man possessed the supreme power of command over the entire Solar Fleet. In the hands of a reasonable man these thousands of ships represented an effective political instrument. But Thomas Cardif was no longer a man of reason. Under his command the fleet was more dangerous to humanity than an uncontrolled nuclear fire.

10 ADVENTURES FROM NOW
You'll cheer the
Savior of the Empire

2/ HARBINGERS OF BLACK DAWN

Thruout the galaxy there are many thousands of confirmations of the law of Cause & Effect. In fact there are countless variables. It often happens that an effect can be produced by 2 practically unrelated causes.

Maj. Albert Kullman did not suspect that his orders were to be *one* of two of the causes for launching 10,000 Arkonide robot-ships. Kullman was commander of one of the patrol cruisers which had penetrated the region of the Arkon Imperium on Cardif's orders. For him the orders were naturally from Rhodan because like any other officer of the Fleet he knew nothing of Cardif's clever masquerade.

Also his character may have played a subordinate role—for the major was overzealous. Under normal circumstances and in a part of the galaxy that belonged to the Solar Imperium, Kullman's concept of duty would have been fully defensible. However, in the middle of a region which an exasperated Imperator of Arkon considered to be rightfully imperial territory, the effect of an officer of Kullman's calibre was like that of a burning fuse in a powder keg.

For 2 days the light cruiser *Zumbasi* had been patrolling the sector assigned to it. The crewmen had been more or less uneasy and disgruntled about this procedure and only Kullman became fully involved with his assignment. He gave talks in the Control Central and pointed to the historical significance of their mission. According to the major it was just a matter of time until the Terrans would take over the Greater Imperium.

Kullman's great moment came when the tracking instruments

of the *Zumbasi* picked up the presence of an alien spaceship which had just emerged from hyperspace. Fortunately it was no problem for the cruiser to reach the vicinity of the other vessel within minutes. Or at least the major considered this to be fortunate.

He was standing now behind Pedro Villaseluces, who was acting as the pilot. Holding a microphone in his hand he watched the viewscreen where the outlines of the other vessel were clearly discernible.

"It's a Springer long-ship, sir," observed Villaseluces sourly. "Those cylindrical hulls are typical of the Galactic Traders."

Kullman's eyes began to gleam. He shouted into the mike, causing the pilot to duck his head between his shoulders. "Attention, Fire Control Center!"

"Sir?" came the response over the speaker.

"Lay a warning shot across the bow of that Springer ship," Kullman ordered. "Do you have it in your sights?"

There was a brief moment of silence. Then came the puzzled voice of Mark Dickson, the Fire Control officer: "You mean—we give them a shot across the bow *before* challenging them to heave to?"

"Do you wish to argue the point with me?" inquired Kullman indignantly.

"No sir but—may I point out to you, sir, that we are in a region where the Springers may do as they please?"

Kullman drew himself up haughtily. "Those times are past, Lt. Dickson. Just keep the Administrator's new orders in mind!"

"Very well, sir," replied Dickson but his tone of voice left no doubt that he didn't think much of Rhodan's new orders.

Kullman could see on the viewscreen that the Springers

seemed uncertain as to how they should react to the spherical warship. They were waiting it out in free fall. Then came a flash from one of the *Zumbasi's* bow guns and an arm-sized bolt of energy shot close across the course of the long-ship.

"Very good, Dickson," said Kullman appreciatively. "That will do for a starter."

Fleming called from the Com Room: "Springer ship requests video contact, sir. Shall I channel it thru to you on the videophone?"

"Yes—hurry it up!" ordered the major.

The normal space vidcom screen lit up and a bearded face became visible. If Albert Kullman had ever seen an agitated expression it was this one. The major observed the Springer commander with obvious satisfaction.

"Do you have any plausible explanation for your action, Terran?" the Springer demanded to know.

"Prepare to take on a prize crew for inspection," announced Kullman drily.

"Do you have any idea of your present position?" countered the other heatedly. "Do you at least know enough about cosmic navigation to realize that you are in the sphere of influence of the Greater Imperium?"

The aspersion cast upon his astronautical capabilities served to kindle Kullman's zeal and goad his ambition. "Which is a region we also control," he retorted arrogantly.

"But we're just a harmless merchant ship! If you're going to harass us in this manner you will be responsible for the consequences. I am appealing to your reason!"

Kullman might have been a fair judge of men but in this case he misinterpreted the Trader's attitude. The major was convinced that the Springer was afraid of an inspection. The fear was probably well-founded. No doubt there were contraband goods on board the long-ship. Kullman did not see the worried faces of his crew nor did he notice Villaseluces when the latter shook his head in dismay. He became totally absorbed in what he thought to be the fulfillment of his duty.

"Dickson!" he yelled into the mike. "Put another charge across his bow so that he'll know we mean what we say!"

Meanwhile the Trader had realized what he was up against. "Alright, Terran," he said in angry resignation, "we're heaving to!"

Kullman nodded his satisfaction and ordered Dickson to hold his fire for the time being. A few minutes later he had gotten a prize crew together and transferred across to the Springer ship in a commuter craft. The Traders stood by grimly during the inspection, knowing that their weapons were no match for a Terran patrol cruiser.

Kullman and his men carefully inspected the alien ship and found nothing that could be considered contraband or even suspicious-looking. Slowly the major had to grudgingly admit to himself that he had really stopped a harmless merchant ship and fired a shot across its bow. But Kullman figured that a Terran officer must not apologize to a Springer commander. In icy tones he ordered his boarding commandoes to return with him.

"You may continue your flight," he told the Springer condescendingly.

The bearded commander didn't bother to answer him.

With the awareness of having deceived himself, Kullman came back on board the *Zumbasi*. However he was still convinced that he had carried out what his new set of orders implied.

The airlock hatch had hardly closed behind the major before the Springer ship sent out a hypercom dispatch in which

Kullman's action was depicted. The message found its way thru several relay stations to Arkon where it happened to join an incoming distress call from another group threatened by Terrans.

The effect of both hypercom messages really lent historical importance to Kullman's mission. But of course this was in a sense that was completely different from what the major had imagined.

* * * *

Imperator Gonozal VIII was the exalted ruler over the Greater Imperium but his reign was a very strange one. Among the decadent Arkonides there was hardly a one who was capable of being helpful to Atlan or standing by him. Without the former robot Regent the attempt of this immortal to consolidate the Imperium again would have been doomed to failure. It was a practical impossibility for one man to encompass the tremendous task of ruling a galactic empire that was light-years in extent. The robot Brain alone was able to encompass the entire complex of countless solar systems, to receive the river of messages from them all and assemble them into a logical overall picture.

In spite of this, Atlan was overburdened. He had always entrusted the smaller problems to the Brain since they were of course the most numerous but in the present confused political situation the Imperator required reports on every minor detail. The fact that a kind of cold war had broken out between Arkon and Terra had made Atlan try to cover all news items concerning what was for the time-being a merely political conflict.

The new relationship with his former ally had been very depressing. He had tried to understand the incomprehensible actions of Perry Rhodan but he could make no more sense out of them than could the totally transformed Solar Administrator himself. The activities of the Solar Fleet within the Greater Imperium had forced Atlan to ask the Akons for help. The mother race of the Arkonides had no cause to be fond of the Terrans. After having received a veiled threat from the false Rhodan, he had promised to send the Akons 1000 modern spaceships in return for their help. Hypno-training was in its full course on the planets of the Blue System. Intelligent and clear-thinking Akons lay under the hoods and contacts of the educational accelerators. In a short length of time Atlan would be able to man a giant fleet with an outstanding army of highly-trained crews.

So the 2 allies had become enemies who now faced each other appraisingly. The obvious hardship and pressure this brought to bear on Arkon would have caused Atlan to attack where any other race was concerned. But Rhodan was his personal friend—or had been until his metamorphosis. Altho the Imperator called them "Barbarians" he harbored a great sympathy for the Terrans.

The logic circuits of the robot Brain had again called for an attack against the impudent Terran ships. Atlan continued to bypass the mammoth Brain's conclusions and to operate on the basis of emotional considerations. He hoped that Perry Rhodan would come to his senses and put an end to this erroneous action.

All units of the Arkonide robot fleet had been placed on emergency standby alert. Atlan had held a number of consultations with high dignitaries, to whom his high-pitched activity was more or less a thorn in the side. At the meetings they talked themselves to exhaustion without arriving at any usable decisions.

In these days Atlan was lonelier than ever before . . .

* * * *

The wall in front of Atlan's desk had the effect of being tiled except that each of the "tile" faces happened to be a video tube. They were all remotely connected to the robot Brain, which utilized these multiple channels for relaying news to him.

A servant robot came into the office and brought the Imperator a steaming cup of some kind of stimulant. As the machine moved across the smooth floor it was almost noiseless. Atlan drew the cup to him without looking up. In general such types of servomechs gave voice to polite expressions during their work but Atlan had ordered this characteristic to be erased from the programs of his personal robots. He considered it nonsense to have one's self addressed with cultured phrases by a machine.

The robot left the room as silently as it had entered.

The visitor who sat beside the Imperator's desk smiled discreetly. Gen. Alter Toseff waited until Atlan had sipped his brew.

"It's a Terran recipe, General," said Gonozal VIII. "You should try it sometime."

Toseff only smiled. "Thank you, Your Eminence. I'm afraid my palate is too accustomed to the delights of Saratan."

Saratan was the Arkonide colonial planet where Gen. Alter Toseff had been representing the interests of the Greater Imperium. He was different from most Arkonides by virtue of his vigor and vitality. In his search for such men, Atlan had located him. The computation sector of the Brain had called all usable officers to Arkon. The selection had been made according to strict specifications yet it had been a let-down for Atlan to find that only 43 men could meet the qualifications. Among the selectees the General had shown the highest number of plus factors. Atlan knew that the Brain's selection had been right again. No traces at all of decadence could be seen in Toseff.

"You may have to go without those delights for some time,

General," announced Atlan. "There are important things for you to do."

"I stand prepared to fight anywhere in the interests of the Greater Imperium," declared Toseff decisively. "Do you have special orders for me, Imperator?"

Atlan turned the cup thoughtfully around in his hands. The General's short-cut snow-white hair contrasted sharply with a complexion that was too dark for an Arkonide. Atlan liked this man—he had good rapport with him and suspected that he could rely on him. In spite of an intensified search the robot Brain had only come up with 43 men with the same characteristics as Toseff.

43—in an entire imperium.

Perry Rhodan had millions of men at his disposal, all of whom were so qualified. This was why Atlan needed the help of the still-vigorous and active Akons. However, he was planning to send an Arkonide of Gen. Toseff's quality to every fleet task force that was to be manned by Akons.

"The assignment you will receive from me can have life or death significance for our Imperium," Atlan revealed. "That's why I am giving you an opportunity to decline the offer—in which case you can then go back to Saratan in *status quo*, the same as when you left it."

"I am at your command, Imperator," said the General. "For generations the Toseffs have stood loyally with the Imperium."

Atlan felt it would be unfair to keep the man in the dark any longer so he shoved an open file toward him across the desk. "Read that," he told him. "In there you will see . . ."

He was interrupted by a buzzer. In front of him on the wall of monitor screens a red light had come on. Toseff looked up and appeared to have forgotten the documents.

"Excuse me a moment," said Atlan. "This is an important

message from the Brain.'' He switched on the communicator unit that was on his desk and another indicator lamp lit up.

An impartial-sounding voice said: ''The high priest of Baalol on Saos requests permission to speak with the Imperator over hypercom transmission.''

Annoyed, Atlan replied: ''I'm busy now. The Anti can wait!''

Undeterred, the mechanical voice continued: ''The matter concerns a new infringement by the Solar Fleet. The Imperator has ordered that every report of this nature shall immediately . . .''

''Alright!'' interrupted Atlan swiftly. ''Let's have the hookup!''

''The priest will speak to you on channel 23,'' came the instruction.

Toseff started to get up and leave but Atlan called to him. ''Wait, General! It can't hurt anything to have you in on this. It definitely is connected with your assignment later.''

Toseff took his seat again. One of the vid-screens on the wall brightened and out of blurred outlines emerged the lean features of the officiating high priest on Saos. The flick of a button by Atlan sufficed to enable the Anti to see a projection of the Imperator's face on the screens in the Control Central of the temple pyramid on Saos. Atlan had no reason for being kindly disposed toward the priests. Even among the planets of the Arkon System they had infiltrated their narcotic liqueur known as Liquitiv.

''What do you want?'' asked the undying admiral coldly.

Kutlos' thin face remained expressionless and only his lips moved as he replied: ''I have an item of news for you, Your Eminence.'' It was as tho the item, in fact, were not of any special interest.

Atlan glanced questioningly at Toseff, then back to the screen. "Speak!" he commanded the Anti.

"The planet Saos belongs to the sovereign territory of the Greater Imperium," said Kutlos calmly.

Atlan became more impatient. "Are you trying to instruct me in astropolitics?" he inquired frostily.

Kutlos smiled. Seldom had Atlan ever seen such a humorless smile. He had to concede that the Anti was an expert in hiding his feelings, if he had any. In the other's cold, angular features there was not the slightest trace of emotion.

"By no means," the priest assured him sarcastically. "But perhaps a lesson in cosmic strategy."

Gen. Toseff harumphed angrily at this impudent remark but Atlan gave him a signal to calm himself. He surmised that the antimutant was merely trying to stage his announcement dramatically.

Nevertheless Kutlos' next statement came as a surprise because of the completely unchanged matter-of-factness in his tone of voice: "Saos is faced with an imminent invasion by a Solar Fleet task force which is under the command of Perry Rhodan."

Atlan started visibly when Perry's name was mentioned, as tho his senses struggled to reject what he had heard. It took him several seconds to recover from the shock. "You are certain that they are Terran ships?" he asked.

"If you hurry you can see for yourself," suggested the Anti with obvious irony. "But don't wait too long because in the meantime Saos could evaporate under a barrage of fusion bombs. At any rate, Rhodan has appeared here with 4000 ships."

"4000 . . . " Atlan repeated the figure gloomily. "He's leading an attack against a planet of the Greater Imperium with a major fleet formation. That is an open act of war!"

For the firsttime Kutlos revealed a spark of intensity. "Will you intervene?" he inquired.

Atlan's answering look was anything but friendly. It was no task to read the priest's mind at the moment. Nevertheless Rhodan's action was a monstrous provocation which in itself was the same as a declaration of war. "Why don't you think about that question?" said Atlan abruptly, and he cut off.

Toseff opened his mouth to say something but desisted when he noticed the Imperator's obvious agitation. He felt instinctively that he was not able to help this lonely man in his decisions now. Yet at the same time the General's loyalty found a still more solid anchorage here. He sensed the rapport between himself and the immortal which also made his devotion to the Greater Imperium indestructible.

"How could the Barbarian do such a thing?" muttered Atlan dejectedly. "Is he using every provocation possible to unleash a galactic war?"

"Perhaps the priest lied to you," suggested the General without too much conviction. "The Baalols might be quite interested in seeing a clash between Terra and Arkon because the 2 powers together are invincible to them."

"Oh, without doubt!" agreed Gonozal VIII. "But I believe the Anti has spoken the truth. He knows only too well that I have the means of checking out his information very swiftly. With a lie he would be risking the existence of the base on Saos."

The General was somewhat alarmed to see that Atlan was hesitating to reply in kind to the aggressive challenge of the Solar Fleet. His friendship with Perry Rhodan seemed to bind him in invisible chains. He could not bring himself to realize that the Earth's First Administrator could break every agreement and treaty in such a manner as this.

"Your Highness," admonished Toseff, "any further hesitance on our part will appear to our allied worlds and especially the rebellious colonies to be a sign of weakness. Also our failure to act will only invite more Terran aggressions. There has to be a limit somewhere. Forgive me for pressing you with these objections.''

Atlan pressed the back of his hand across his forehead. The silence in the large room seemed oppressive to Toseff. There was also a pervading chilliness altho it could have been his imagination.

''I thank you for your frankness, General,'' Atlan answered earnestly. ''I like it when somebody speaks an opinion straight out with no flowery attachments. As you well know, that's very rare for our 'dignitaries' in the Council.''

''They would have a hard time arriving at a decision, Imperator,'' said the representative from Saratan.

Atlan smiled humorlessly. ''There's an old Arkonide proverb that the closer one gets to a breakup of friendships the more patience one must have. But how much patience *is* that, General?''

Atlan's question expressed the entire extent of the situation. While attempting on the one hand to avoid an open break with Rhodan he was occupied simultaneously on the other hand with the task of using every means at his disposal to protect the Greater Imperium against further military encroachments.

Who could say whether or not Atlan might have still considered his friendship with the Terrans—if it had not been for a certain Maj. Albert Kullman?

Just as Toseff was about to voice an opinion, the robot Brain buzzed and flashed another emergency signal, requesting a connection with Atlan. The General interrupted himself and waited while the Imperator worked his control buttons.

The same monotonous voice came from the speakers: ''A further infringement of the Solar Fleet in the sovereign territory of the Greater Imperium has been reported. A hypercom message from a Springer ship has just been received. A Terran warship fired upon the merchant ship and ordered it to stop. A prize crew then boarded the Trader vessel and proceeded to subject it to inspection. Sonzomon, the Springer commander, is demanding reparations and a public apology from the Terran officer in charge.''

Atlan interrupted the connection to his mechanical aide with the flat of his hand. His lips had thinned out to a sliver. "*That* is how far the patience goes!" he said coldly. "You stack it high enough and something's going to make it crash. This is it!''

"So, Your Highness?" Toseff watched him intently.

Atlan pulled a star map from a nearby chart rack and spread it out on the desk. The General leaned forward and studied it as Atlan took a marker and drew a circle around star cluster M-13. All the Arkonide colonial planets had been previously marked with red dots. Atlan's outstretched finger pointed to one of them.

"Here!" he said.

"What is your plan, Sire?" asked Toseff. The star chart drew him strangely as tho here at this moment were new signs and symbols of historical destiny.

"The time has passed, once and for all, General, in which we will take any more from the barbarians of Earth. Arkon is striking back. We will stand for no further encroachments without retaliating!" These words of war were virtually shouted by Atlan. "Our Akon allies are still under the hypno-training process and can't be put to use yet. This means that we'll have to launch a robot fleet. It can match the Terrans in fire power but can't react as fast or come up with all the amazing trickery that Rhodan's men always employ during a cosmic space battle.''

The Arkonide from Saratan tensed as he asked his next question: "Imperator, do you wish to send a fleet to rescue Saos?"

Atlan's fist slammed down on the map target. "10,000 ships should be enough," he said.

"Ten—thousand . . .?!" echoed Toseff, stammering in surprise.

"Further formations will be placed on standby for backup," declared the immortal admiral. "If Rhodan wants to conjure up a test of power, then he shall have it!"

The General gazed silently at the map. In his mind's eye he had a picture of the 10,000 Arkonide robotships bursting out of hyperspace upon the astonished Terrans. It was something to rekindle the vision of the Imperium's former splendor. He saw the names and faces of the great ones of previous generations passing before him. His eyes gleamed when he recalled such legendary figures as Ufagar, Salaston and Petesch III.

True, the Imperium had been scarred and wounded, it was splintered and torn, but it was still much more than an empty concept. At its head stood a determined man who was ready to use every means at his command to prevent a collapse.

"We shall defeat them, Imperator!" Toseff cried. "We'll sweep them out of the Greater Imperium and teach them such a lesson that they'll never dare come back again!"

Atlan shook his head. "Now you're speaking like a Terran, General," he said softly. "If, however, you can manage to *operate* like a Terran you'll know how hard it is to overcome them. They have an iron will not to be stopped by anything. This forward-striving compulsion is symbolized by just one man."

"Perry Rhodan," added Toseff.

"Who strikes him down gives a deadly blow to Terra," said Atlan. He pressed a button and the servant robot came in quietly—so soundlessly in fact that it startled Toseff. "My conference with Leschtos must be postponed indefinitely," Atlan reported to the robot. "I deeply regret that he has had to come this far in vain."

Toseff quickly caught the significance of this instruction. "Does that mean, Your Eminence, that you are going to accompany the Fleet?"

The Imperator chuckled briefly. "Just you and I as the only active Arkonides—leading the mechanical crews of 10,000 robotships. How does that strike you, General?"

Toseff smiled. Altho a veteran warrior with much experience, he had still preserved a healthy sense of humor. "As quite promising," he answered.

3 minutes later, Atlan made contact with the Brain. Positronic programming circuits began to work at top speed. It was necessary to find the most strategic attack approach for lifting the siege of Saos. Meanwhile, Atlan made preparations for taking command of the flagship. Toseff was bubbling over with ideas. He was faster than the giant Arkon "think tank" in working out a battle plan.

* * * *

Thousands of light-years distant, Maj. Albert Kullman sat in his command chair on board the light cruiser *Zumbasi* and spoke confidently to his pilot, Villaseluces. "I think we handled that situation correctly. Now the Springers know they can't get thru any part of the galaxy without being checked. It will be a constructive warning to them." He leaned back into the pliant upholstery with a sense of satisfaction.

In that same instant a certain relay clicked in the robot Brain on Arkon 3. A directional signal beam was automatically transmitted. Minutes later the mighty impulse engines of 10,000 Arkonide warships thundered into life. They were harbingers of a black dawn in the history of the galaxy.

A tragic collision was threatened between 2 mighty fleets.

3/ THE GAME OF DEATH

Cardif's fingers clutched at the place where he knew the cell activator to be in his bloated chest. The Antis had lured him into the trap of procuring this device. It did not occur to Cardif's tortured mind that *It*, the multiple being on Wanderer, could have had something to do with this change of his cells. He had never comprehended the ambiguous warning nor did he see its significance now.

He would never understand it. The cell division was proportional in every part of his body. His brain had been affected as much as any other organ. Cardif's mental condition was such that he no longer even recognized the danger of a betrayal of his identity by the Antis. Blindly he relied on his plan of revenge which would place the planet Saos in his hands. There he hoped to obtain the information necessary for his cure.

He would show the men that he still knew how to command a fleet. He finally groaned and rolled out of the rumpled bed. He ran his hands testingly over the sweater he was wearing. The loose pullover seemed to be filling out. Was it becoming too tight already?

He changed his trousers and put his hair in order. Disdainfully he threw the dark goggles aside. Why should he, the Administrator, have to hid his face? Let the officers see the eyes of the man who would lead them to victory over the Antis. Cardif giggled softly in anticipation. The time of waiting was over. He had permitted Bell's admonishments to hold him back much too long. Later when he had consolidated his power, Bell would be one of the first to be liquidated.

Cardif double-checked his appearance. He did not wish to acknowledge his inner desperation and panic. He was preparing once more to act the part of Administrator of the Solar Imperium—a role that suited him less and less.

His appearance in the Control Central was met with various reactions. The comportment of the false Rhodan had placed the officers of the *Ironduke* under a very unusual strain. As Cardif stopped just inside the entrance hatchway and stood there looking searchingly at the men, his arms akimbo, he sensed their instinctive rejection of him. He drew himself to his full height and noticed that his hair brushed the upper frame of the doorway. It meant he had grown that much more in the meantime.

Then he stepped forward into the room and barked a command at Jefe Claudrin. "General orders to all ships, Colonel. We will begin the attack against Saos."

Claudrin heaved his ponderous bulk around and moved thru the Control Central like a human tank. Over regular spacecom he established contact with the task force commanders. "Maybe it would be better, sir, if you spoke to them yourself," he suggested quietly. "That would give them a boost for the forthcoming battle."

Thomas Cardif's grin of derision revealed again that he was losing his father's touch. In fact his voice was almost corrosive in its mockery. "For a conquest of this ridiculous little base, Colonel, *your* voice will be more than sufficient!"

"Very well, sir." Without further comment, the Epsalian-born commander carried out his instructions.

Cardif looked at the ship's chronometer. "In precisely 1 hour, Terra time," he said, "the first ships of our fleet will land on Saos."

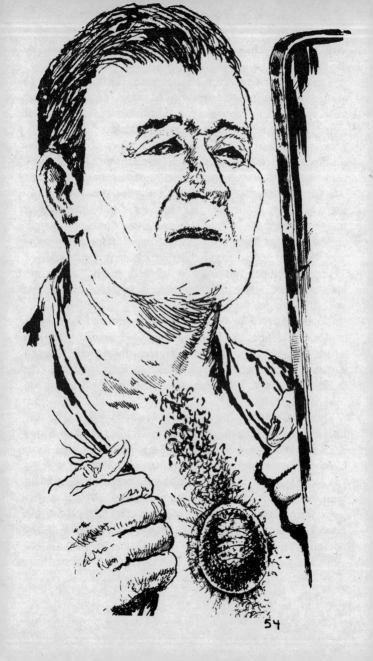

"I can't help it, Perry," said Bell from his flight seat, "but I have an uneasy feeling about this show. The Antis are suspiciously quiet."

Cardif broke out into a shrill laugh as his bloated features twisted in a grimace of defiance. Most of the officers lowered their gaze or looked away to avoid the wild expression in the Administrator's eyes. But it was also clear to the last man on board the *Ironduke* that Rhodan would never abandon his purpose.

In monotonous tones, Jefe Claudrin communicated with the other ships. The commanders received their instructions calmly. Not one of them voiced any objections. Now as before, their confidence in the Rhodan personality was still unshakable.

"No one can stop us!" shouted Cardif. "We will smoke out this rat's nest!"

He still did not know how badly he had deceived himself.

* * * *

From whatever angle Kutlos regarded his conversation with Gonozal VIII he could not see that the results were very satisfactory. The Imperator had not shown anywhere near the amount of reaction that Kutlos had hoped for. The high priest realized that he had made a mistake in having irritated the immortal unnecessarily. It had only served to increase the Imperator's antipathy toward the Antis. It was now highly questionable whether or not at least a portion of the Arkon Fleet would fight for Saos.

He sat in the chair that was designated for his lofty station and was lost in thought while shreds of conversation from the other Antis filtered thru his consciousness. Nowhere was there a trace of optimism to be detected. Everyone knew that in case of an attack by the Terran ships there could be no hope of rescue. The defeat on Okul had proved that the priests' individual defense screens were no longer effective against the men of Earth.

A cry of alarm rang out: "The Terran ships are changing their positions!"

It startled Kutlos out of his thoughts and it took him a second or two to become reoriented. The priests were crowding in front of the mass-energy detection consoles.

"Let me thru!" he demanded. His lean figure moved among them, shoving them roughly out of the way.

The glowing green tracking blips were in motion. Their deployment positions were forming an unmistakable pattern. Kutlos didn't have to be clairvoyant to know what this change signified. His face darkened. The invasion was about to begin.

Tasnor blurted out a bitter accusation: "Your plan has failed, Kutlos! They are attacking before Gonozal VIII can help us. I still doubt that he will even show up here with his ships."

The high priest realized that the younger man's harsh criticism was merely an outward expression of his fear of death. It would have been senseless to argue with him.

Meanwhile Hepna-Kaloot had climbed onto one of the chairs and was waving his arms for attention. Kutlos regarded this as an infringement upon his own authority but he did not protest. The stubby little priest's action would help to distract the others from Tasnor's panicky rebellion.

"Now there is no doubt that all of us must die!" declared Hepna-Kaloot. There was something in his little beady eyes that aroused more curiosity in Kutlos than anger so he continued to maintain his silence. "Should we wait for the Terrans to kill us one after the other?" continued the chubby one. As he paused for effect, Kutlos began to have a presentiment of what he was leading up to.

But that would be absurd, he thought. He can't possibly mean *that!* Could he be mistaken or was Hepna-Kaloot eyeing him scornfully? There was something about the little man now that momentarily blocked his resolve. Somehow he couldn't pull himself together to warn the priest and forbid him to speak.

"Only animals *wait* for death!" shouted Hepna-Kaloot. His chin shot forward and Kutlos began to see in him the signs of a deeply-rooted brutality. It startled him more than the awareness of the impending invasion by the Solar Fleet. "Until the end comes, let's use the time like men! Let two fighters draw lots for the game of Paloot!"

Kutlos closed his eyes momentarily but the shouts of approval from the other priests stunned him out of his paralysis. Hepna-Kaloot climbed down from the chair and moved among the excited men. The high priest was aware of cold sweat on his brow. Tasnor, standing to one side, looked forlorn. His attack against his superior had been without effect. It was Hepna-Kaloot who dominated the situation.

"Stop!" shouted Kutlos.

The group of men in their wide capes separated to reveal the fat little priest who was already preparing the lots.

"The game is forbidden!" the high priest warned them but he was aware of striving to make his voice sound convincing.

Hepna-Kaloot threw the first lot to him. "Who will call us to account when we're dead?" he challenged.

Kutlos caught the lot and broke it in his hands. "It is forbidden!" he insisted stubbornly. He wished he could offer further reasons against it but couldn't think of any.

"The High Priest withdraws from the game!" said Hepna-Kaloot scornfully. "That means only *one* fighter is to be chosen—and I volunteer myself!"

Kutlos had once believed that nothing could make him lose his temper but at the moment he couldn't help himself. He fumed inwardly with rage as he regarded the stocky little priest warily. In Hepna-Kaloot's eyes he could see a silent question.

Kutlos heard himself speak altho his hands were trembling: "No contenders need to be chosen. I will go against Hepna-Kaloot!"

Hepna-Kaloot seemed to have expected nothing else. Unhesitatingly he began to remove his outer garments.

"Wait!" said the high priest. "I am not familiar with the rules!"

The stocky priest smiled. "When we fight to the limit of Taloosei, nothing is barred!"

"Then we might as well begin," said Kutlos. "Let's choose the referee. I nominate Egtoor."

It was agreeable to Hepna-Kaloot. Egtoor looked doubtfully at the high priest.

"Who will begin with the choice of weapons?" he asked uncertainly.

The first to choose had a disadvantage because the opponent could then select weapons more suitable for his defense. Of course the second to choose could not select a weapon already named.

"I'm in favor of each contender choosing 3 weapons," suggested Hepna-Kaloot. "If the high priest agrees, I will begin." It was an offer that advertised Hepna-Kaloot's low estimation of Kutlos' fighting capabilities. "I will take a monitor-spy, a Sostoos knife and a water can."

To the high priest the monitor-spy was a shrewd selection but what Hepna-Kaloot expected to do with the water can was beyond him. Nor was the knife an unusually dangerous weapon. But at least he knew that he himself could not avail himself of a monitor-spy.

"I'll take an energy gun, a Lagoo rope . . . " Kutlos hesitated. "And Tasnor as my runner."

A runner was the only means of counteracting the advantage of the remote spy device. Tasnor accepted his choice as "weapon #3" in silence. Hate flamed in his eyes but he could not refuse to be the runner. Altho Tasnor could not himself attack, he would be in continuous danger. Hepna-Kaloot would be free to use any and all weapons against him. It would only be a question of how dangerous he might consider Tasnor to be as a runner against him. Kutlos was hoping that his second-in-command would give Hepna-Kaloot enough trouble to ease his own burden in the battle. But of course there was also the possibility that the belligerent little priest would disregard the runner entirely and come directly against Kutlos himself.

"The contest promises to be interesting," said Hepna-Kaloot. "Too bad it will be a short one. The high priest does not have my experience."

This was an open confession that he had taken part before in the forbidden game of Paloot.

"I've gone as far as the Taloosei seven times already," he said proudly. "How often I've played the tamer versions I can't even say. *Too* often for you, Kutlos!"

The cutting challenge served to steady the high priest's mind, bringing back his cool calculation. He only turned his gaze from his opponent to Tasnor, his runner. The latter's face was pale but he removed his outer garments. Agtlos went with Egtoor to get the weapons.

As first chooser, Hepna-Kaloot started out. He carried the water can in his right hand. The heavy dagger protruded from the belt of his skin-tight trousers. Above his head floated the monitor eye. The receiver and transmitting gear hung over one shoulder. In the little viewscreen provided, it would be possible for him to follow Kutlos' movements unless the latter succeeded in destroying the "spy" part of the equipment.

"Luck to you, Hepna-Kaloot," said Egtoor, according to the tradition of the game.

"Follow him!" Kutlos ordered his unhappy runner. "I want

continuous reports on his position. I also have to find out what he intends to do with that water!''

He holstered the energy gun and draped the Lagoo rope over his shoulder. Now he was prepared.

''Why do you not remove your cape, Kutlos?'' asked Egtoor.

''It is the cape of a high priest,'' Kutlos replied with dignity. ''I've worn it too long now to remove it merely for this.''

He could see in the priests' faces what they were thinking. He had lived his life in this cape and he would fight his battles in it—even should Hepna-Kaloot force him into the deadly phase of Taloosei.

Taloosei had no equivalent in translation altho it came close

to what Japanese had once called *kamikaze*—except that this was suicide out of desperation. So it was that in its deadliest form the game of Paloot must end with the death of one of the contenders.

Tasnor went soundlessly out of the temple's Control Central. And now it was time for Kutlos to be on his way as well. He drew himself up gravely and headed for the exit but before he reached it the hypersensors set up a shrill sound of alarm. Transition shockwaves! Kutlos came to a stop abruptly. It couldn't be true, he thought—he couldn't be so lucky!

"Kutlos!" cried an excited voice.

He turned about and returned to his companions. The tracking blips representing the Terran ships had come to rest. The reason for it became clearly apparent immediately. At least 10,000 ships had emerged from hyperspace and were hurtling into the Saos System. These were not Solar Imperium forces. Kutlos had to support himself on the console with both hands in order not to stagger in the transport of relief he felt.

"They are coming!" he shouted, beside himself. "The Imperator is coming to our aid!"

A jubilant cheer drowned him out. The sensor equipment shook physically under the impact of the heavy shocks it was registering. In fact the building itself was trembling slightly. This meant that the mass formation had emerged from transition dangerously close to the planet. The colossal discharges of warp energy were enough to send seismic shockwaves thru the shell of Saos itself.

Kutlos was filled with an incomparable sense of triumph. His strategy had won a new victory. The greatest of them all! Now it was only a question of time before the 2 great fleets would be in conflict with one another.

From the entrance of the chamber came a rasping sound.

Kutlos looked up. He stared incredulously at the thing that was hovering there halfway between floor and ceiling. It was Hepna-Kaloot's spy monitor.

Either the other priest had not been informed of the turn of events or he was desperately determined to keep his game alive. Just for a moment Kutlos had deviated from his fixed policy of following High Council strategy and the result was this senseless fight with Hepna-Kaloot. Kutlos long-awaited battle of Titans in outer space was to have its tiny counterpart here on Saos.

The hovering electronic eye left no doubt that Hepna-Kaloot had made the first move.

Kutlos reached unobtrusively for his beamer. The monitor seemed to weave back and forth above the entrance like an insect blinded by the light. Somewhere Hepna-Kaloot lay in ambush, waiting for his antagonist. On his micro-screen he could follow every movement the high priest made.

Kutlos whipped out his weapon and fired just as the apparatus ducked beneath his aim. The searing beam bored a black hole in the wall. The spy-eye swept out of the room and was gone. The tracking sensors were making an undulating racket in response to the swift approach of the Arkonide fleet. Now the spherical ships of the Terrans were showing activity again. The blockade ring opened up its tight formation. For a moment Kutlos thought the Solar Fleet was going to make a run for it but it soon became apparent that the various units were merely changing position.

Tasnor came in. His hair was dangling in his face. He looked at Kutlos and thru him as tho still envisioning his recent ordeal. "Hepna-Kaloot is in Energy Station 3," he reported tonelessly. "The sham attack of the Springers has practically destroyed the place. He is hiding in the ruins." His eyes suddenly widened. "He came after me with the knife!"

Kutlos nodded grimly. His thin, sunken features hardened. He would have to pay for his triumph here. He took one last look at the viewscreens. The master plan was unfolding.

"Keep him under surveillance!" he ordered.

The deputy high priest went away to carry out his macabre task. Kutlos felt no compassion for the youngster. He was too busy thinking of the triumph of the plan—and of Hepna-Kaloot on the other hand, who waited to engage him in the death play of Taloosei.

When he left the Control Central of the temple he went resignedly to pay the price he knew he must pay—for having deserted the strategy of Great Baalol for even a single moment. Tall, lean, with stiff and measured tread, he exited the main observation center while clutching his energy weapon so tightly that his knuckles were white.

There would be no returning.

25 ADVENTURES FROM NOW
Perhaps you'll agree that
A Dead One Should Not Die

4/ DOOMSDAY SHUFFLE

When Gen. Alter Toseff finally recovered from the pains of transition he saw that the Imperator was already standing in front of the tracking and sensor consoles of the flagship. As he shook himself and got up from his convertible flight seat, Atlan turned to look at him.

"The priest was not lying. At least 4000 ships have been deployed around Saos. By their present positions I'd say they are up to their ears in preparations for an invasion."

The mass-sensor instruments were showing a maximum registration. Thousands of tracking blips swarmed across the sweep-screens like fireflies and the energy-scopes were going wild with peak gyrations while on the viewscreen the crescent outline of Saos stood out in a firmament of ships—not stars. The planet's gravitational tendrils were plucking now at the Arkonide ships but the super-powerful impulse engines went into a braking mode which handled the pull with ease.

Atlan knew that at the moment it would be senseless to take command of the 10,000 robotships which were presently under control of their separate positronicons. Over translight data links, each was in contact with the robot Brain of Arkon. All inputs were handled simultaneously, processed within seconds for total strategic evaluation, and the giant Brain piloted them all accordingly. Even on the flagship itself Atlan had left the navigation to the autopilot system.

The ancient but ever-youthful Admiral did not intend to attack without warning. He was certain the Brain was placing the ships into attack positions but once that was accomplished it would automatically interrogate him. Without his specific direction, not one Arkonide shot would be fired. The robot fleet was an ultimate threat and Rhodan would understand it as such. Atlan was still hoping to work out something with his friend on the basis of reason.

Toseff was watching the screens closely. "Your Eminence, they don't seem to have landed on the planet as yet," he advised.

"They are holding up the landing maneuver," replied Atlan. "They spotted us immediately. Now let them scratch their heads a little, to see how they can manage to handle 10,000 ships at their backs while they're facing the ground defenses of the Saos stronghold."

The Arkonide from Saratan pondered this statement. "Let's hope they don't think of one of their famous tricks that you give them so much credit for."

Atlan smiled gravely. "We have them on a leash. They're sharp enough to see their position. It won't be long now before they'll be trying to have a palaver."

For the General this whole situation brought with it a prickling sense of new awakening. He had spent most of his life on Saratan, a small fruitful planet with gently-rolling hills and gentler beasts with furry pelts and large, wondering eyes. Looking back in his thoughts he found it incredible that he could have been satisfied with his existence there. He suddenly saw Saratan as the pastureland for old men who wished to fade away in blissful dreaming.

In astonishment he reflected that he had not realized this sooner. But for the present incident he might have spent his last days lying in a lotus bed. At last Toseff knew the meaning of his frequent spells of restlessness. It had been nothing more than the outward expression of an unconscious compulsion, his search for another field of activity.

As the General gazed at the quarter crescent of this alien world before him, he thought he must be dreaming. "Farewell, Saratan," he said softly.

If the Imperator heard him he made no comment. Old Toseff took a deep breath. Was it an evil compulsion that awakened in him the battle urge? Or was it just a natural reaction? Something had been dammed up within him that pressed now insistently for release.

He stood silently beside Atlan and watched the developments on the screens. The Terran ships were still changing their positions but now it was clearly evident that the attack configuration was breaking up. Instead, the spherical vessels of the Solar Fleet were regrouping into a typical defensive pattern. Three heavy ships formed an advance guard for each of the groups while 8 other units kept in motion around them, more or less forming a cone in terms of spatial geometry. The flanks of each cone were made up of smaller and faster cruisers.

Toseff could visualize the effectiveness of such formations. In case of enemy attack the 3 advance ships could thrust forward with lightning swiftness and attempt to "wedge" thru the attacking phalanx. Of course in most cases the daring ones in front would have to face the worst losses but the incoming opponent would be so busy with the flying wedges that he would not be able to concentrate sufficiently on the rest of the group. And here would be the decisive part of the battle since the flanking escorts, in spite of their smaller size, were noted for their considerable striking power.

The Terran commanders were gradually forming countless defense cones around Saos.

"They've been forced into defensive tactics," Atlan observed with grim satisfaction. "That should make them more ready to talk business."

Secretly he was not overly convinced of this, however. He had merely expressed what he fervently wished. Terrans had always been notoriously hard-headed and unapproachable when anybody pushed them for a capitulation. But that was precisely the purpose of these advancing 10,000 warships of Arkon.

Saos itself was a worthless planet. It would represent no economic loss to the Greater Imperium. It was military prestige alone that was at stake here. Atlan could not permit alien fleet units to enter his stellar domain and start attacking planets. For the sake of survival he had to maintain face among his countless internal allies and all the colonial worlds.

With a heavy heart Atlan made contact with the former robot Regent, which was being of incalculable service to him now. "Hold all ships in attack position," he ordered calmly. "All weapons batteries in combat readiness. I will issue further instructions directly to all robot units."

The mammoth positronicon confirmed the message, after which Atlan turned to Gen. Toseff. In the bright illumination of the command consoles he could see the sensitive little lines that were etched in the features of the Saratan officer.

"We'll give them 30 minutes to make contact with us," he said.

In Toseff's eyes was an unspoken but obvious question.

"Then we attack!"

For Atlan these words were no longer part of his troubled dreams. In this bitter hour they had emerged into hard reality.

* * * *

Thomas Cardif sensed the continuous deterioration of his mind. He could follow the process as clearly as if it were being projected on a screen before him. More and more his primitive instincts were overriding logic and reason. His long, bellowing outburst when the Arkonide ships emerged from hyperspace, his reckless order for an immediate attack which Bell had to struggle hard to talk him out of—all this pointed to the fact that he was losing his powers of judgment.

He fought against the encroaching mental disability, forcing himself where he could to act with discernment and to express himself more objectively. Yet every time the fragile veneer of reason was shattered by his more brutal instincts, by the uprooting of his psyche and these despotic fits of temperament. More and more Cardif was becoming the prisoner of a split personality.

On the other hand the silent concern of his officers and the serious looks that were being exchanged in the tense atmosphere on board the *Ironduke* were not conducive to calming his nerves. He was more sensitive than a wounded bull. The most diplomatic criticism was enough to make him lose his head.

With burning eyes he watched the viewscreens where it became clearly evident that the Arkonide ships were lining up for an attack. Against the blackness of the outer void they were like so many pearls being carefully threaded onto imaginary strings.

"That force must contain at least 10,000 ships," Bell remarked. It was merely a technical observation but Cardif thought his stocky deputy was trying to give him a warning.

"So what!" he fumed. "They can't stop me!" He looked down at himself and pulled at his sweater to adjust it. "I want the robots to get me a new uniform jacket immediately," he growled, "and this time I want one that fits! If this self-inflated star king wants to deal with me, I'm going to face him with full dress and rank!"

Bell's skeptical glance informed him that no one was going to expect Atlan to make the first move in a radio contact. The officers thought it much more likely that the Arkonide admiral was waiting for Rhodan to do the calling.

Maj. Krefenbac passed on the order for a new uniform jacket. So far Cardif had not made any further attempt to replace the First Officer with another man.

Bell took another look at the tracking indicators and seemed to be momentarily relieved. "It doesn't look as if they're planning to jump us right away," he said. "They're holding their present positions."

"A lousy swarm of gnats!" shouted Cardif, burning with hate.

He paced rapidly back and forth in front of the hypersensor panels like a caged animal. He had a hunted look. He was now taller than any man on board. A horrible change was becoming apparent in his features. The recognizable outlines of his face were fading in a mass of shapeless flesh. His skin was becoming visibly porous—an effect which became more prominent as he broke out into a sweat. Only his eyes gave a semblance of character to his dissolving countenance but they were the yellow-gleaming eyes of a carnivorous cat. They dominated the bloated mass like 2 smouldering orbs in a desolate wasteland. The man whom everyone took for Perry Rhodan was turning into a monstrosity whose very appearance was upsetting to those around him.

"They're a little nastier than gnats," insinuated Col. Claudrin. "If Atlan gives the order to attack we won't be able to hold out very long against a mass assault by those robotships."

By now it had become impossible for the Epsalian commander to read the Administrator's reactions in that swollen face. It was very disconcerting to him. He was accustomed to detecting

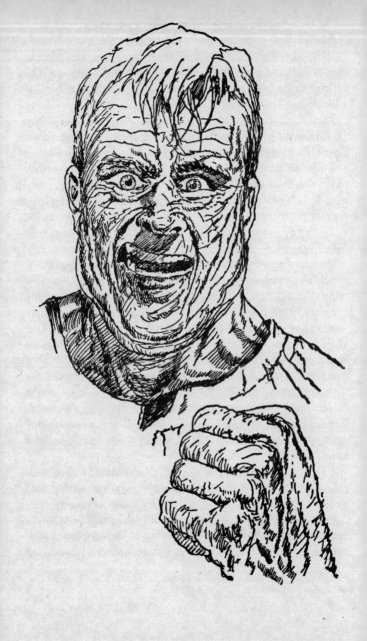

the secret thoughts of anyone he was talking to by their facial reactions. Not that Rhodan's face was expressionless by any means but its present contortions could hardly be interpreted. For Claudrin that jerking of puffed-up flesh and the barely detectable tensing of the now flabby skin transmitted little or nothing to him.

As for the colonel's own physiology, he was not typically human. The heavier gravity of Epsal had developed him into a man who was more like a walking grizzly. Claudrin was almost as wide as he was tall, which was not much over 5 feet. Nevertheless his appearance was not repugnant. His physical structure had adapted itself to the natural conditions of his native planet. From an Epsalian's viewpoint the Terrans themselves were somewhat ''deformed'', like many other humanoid intelligences. After all, toads might seem repugnant to humans but perhaps for lack of speech the latter creatures could not express how ugly their beholders seemed to them. The question of beauty—or its opposite, ugliness—was thus a relative matter which could only be judged within each species or type, and only there.

To a Terran maiden, Jefe Claudrin might have seemed to be a clumsy-looking oaf, whereas an Epsalian girl—being almost as broad as the colonel—might have been carried away by his splendid appearance.

But Rhodan's repulsiveness was not in any category but its own. Members of his own species had to consider him now as a physical abnormality. Certain types of birds on Earth were known to kill their deformed young and cast them out of the nest without mercy. Every species including the human race had an instinctive prejudice against deformitites within their own phylum. By the laws of Nature, of course, such an attitude was all a part of the built-in compulsion toward survival thru natural selection. However, the human mind alone, by virtue of its unique ability to think independently, had fortunately improved upon Nature with laws of its own—such as tolerance and equality.

Yet in human emotions the instinctive uneasiness remained. Goodwill and compassion failed to camouflage the fact that the Frankenstine complex was inextinguishable in human nature. A person scarred by burns might awaken pity yet only the victim realized how obviously he was shunned. Altho humans did not kill the deformed of their kind, perhaps they committed unconsciously something that was much more horrible: psychologically they ostracized such objects of pity by avoiding contact with them.

The officers of the *Ironduke* were also human, governed by feelings and emotions. Gradually Rhodan was becoming one of the psychologically ostracized—an alien thing. The worse his deformity became, the greater was their pity, accompanied by the wish to be separated from this creature.

Himself a model of human tolerance, Jefe Claudrin was aware of the wall that was growing between him and Rhodan. Rhodan was going thru a metamorphosis that made him appear to be inhuman—or at least he was no longer human in the traditional sense. To put it another way, what was happening to him was not a *human* change.

Cardif interrupted his deck-pacing in front of the consoles. "Atlan's trying to intimidate us," he said suddenly. "He's putting the pressure on, hoping he can make us come crawling! He's in for an unpleasant surprise—isn't that right, Bell?" He practically bellowed the last few words.

Bell's deadly earnest expression remained unchanged. His voice was strangely husky when he spoke. "Atlan has more than twice our own firing power. Under the circumstances I say it's suicide to try landing on Saos, because that's all the Arkonides will let it come to—a *try!*"

Cardif only laughed. "I'm going back to my cabin," he announced. "When the robots are ready with my new uniform, then I'll be ready to talk to Atlan." He hastily left the Control Central.

Col. Claudrin cleared his throat for attention. "Excuse me, sir," he said, turning to Bell. "I see our present situation as purely untenable. Strategically we're at the bottom of the hill. If the Arkonides start blasting—they'll simply burn us out."

Bell nodded glumly. At the moment they were in a high-stake gamble with a low-card hand. There was no chance of bluffing here because a shavetail space cadet could look at their hemmed-in formations and see thru every play.

"We can only hope that . . ." Bell was interrupted by an excited shout from Maj. Krefenbac.

"Sir—the radio! Somebody's hailing us on ordinary vidcom!"

Rhodan's First Deputy dashed to the console and flipped on voice-video reception while everyone looked at the videoscreen tensely. They were all hoping to see the distinctive features of Atlan.

But it was not the immortal Admiral who was hailing the *Ironduke*. The man who appeared was baldheaded except for a sparse ring of hair around the sides. His intelligent face was shadowed by deep concern.

"Mercant!" exclaimed Bell in amazement. "How the devil did *you* get here!"

"Maybe with these 10,000 ships milling around over your heads you missed our little warp-shock on the sensors," explained the Chief of Solar Intelligence. "I've just been granted safe conduct thru Atlan's lines. At present I am on board the fast cruiser *Acapulco*, commanded by Maj. Burggraf."

Somehow Mercant's presence here was a relief to Bell. The little man was one of Rhodan's closest confidants. Perhaps his

73

influence might still serve to save the situation. "Allan," he said warmly, "I'm sure glad you're here!"

Mercant grinned. "I don't think this cruiser's going to shift the balance of power in this sector of space."

"So you've already noted that Arkon's robotships are not here to support us?"

"That's been rather drastically impressed upon me," said Mercant. With his typical self-composure he sounded as tho he were discussing a Sunday picnic. "We scraped thru under the impulse batteries of the giant flagship and a certain Gen. Toseff was looking down our throats, under orders from Atlan. I presume the Imperator is also on board with him." Mercant smiled. "Apparently we were permitted to join your camp because we weren't considered to be very dangerous."

Col. Claudrin had been watching the approach of the *Acapulco* on his screens. "We'll shuttle you over, sir," he offered.

"Very well," said Mercant. "Maj. Burggraf feels that the Arkonides granted us safe passage because they're sure we'll never make it back—if this powder keg explodes."

"The major may have a point there," said Bell. "Perry won't be budged from his plan to attack the Antis on Saos. "He's . . . " He hesitated. "But it's best for you to see for yourself."

"You mean his physical alteration is continuing," Mercant guessed. A shadow of tragedy touched his already worried features.

"Not only *physical*, Mercant."

"I understand." For a moment or two the man who held in his hand's the galaxy's most gigantic Intelligence machine was seen to close his eyes. Finally he said: "You don't have to shuttle me over. Major Berggraf has just informed me a space-jet is ready. I'll come across to the *Ironduke*. Then we'll confer to see what can be done to stop this thing.''

"Alright, Mercant," Bell agreed.

The Security Chief's face faded from the screen. But there was a new glimmer of hope now that they might still find a way out of a very blind alley.

* * * *

When Allan D. Mercant entered the Control Central of the *Ironduke* he looked questioningly at the assembled officers. "Where is *he?*" he asked.

"In his cabin," Bell told him. "He's waiting for the robots to finish his new uniform because his old one got too tight for him. When he faces Atlan he wants to be in the full brass of a First Administrator."

"Strange," commented the baldheaded chief of Intelligence. "I can't remember when Rhodan ever thought the uniform made the man."

"He's changed his thinking in a lot of ways," said Bell without any particular rancor. "Sometimes it seems that the Chief has turned into a completely different person."

Bell had never come so close to the truth. He still did not harbor the slightest suspicion of Cardif-Rhodan yet he was definitely aware of this change in his friend's inner nature. There was hardly anyone who knew Rhodan better than Bell.

"One day he will get over all this," said Mercant hopefully. "But in the meantime we have to run interference for humanity if we're going to block an irretrievable calamity."

Dr. Riebsam was the logical type who couldn't avoid the obvious. He pointed to the viewscreens and other indicators. "And what would you call *that*, sir?"

"We'll have to talk to Atlan," said Mercant decisively. "What do you think, Bell?"

Bell tightened his lips perplexedly and ran a hand thru his short red hair while Mercant watched him expectantly.

"You mean—go ahead on our own, without telling Perry?"

The Security Chief spread out his arms. For a man his hands were carefully manicured. As always he wore his simple uniform. "What else can we do? The Imperator has to be told about the Chief's condition. That might hold off his attack."

"I agree with you, sir!" rumbled Jefe Claudrin. His leathery hide seemed to flush with excitement. Here was the chance everybody had been waiting for.

In the final analysis, however, it all depended upon Bell's decision. He and Mercant would have to carry the responsibility for such an action.

Bell was troubled. "When the First Administrator is on board a ship he's automatically the commander. In fact he's Commander-in-Chief of this whole fleet. All orders have to come from him. If he finds out that we've gone behind his back . . . " He left the statement dangling.

"I understand your apprehension." Mercant raised his voice slightly. "Nevertheless we should risk it. After all, Rhodan hasn't given any order that *prevents* us from speaking to the Admiral."

"Perry figures that Atlan must open the palaver," Bell reminded everyone. He turned to Maj. Krefenbac. "Major, find out when the robots will be finished with that uniform."

Krefenbac switched on the intercom and connected himself with the appropriate department. After a few seconds he reported: "It will still take awhile, sir."

"I don't like a decision like this," said Bell in a low tone. "It seems to have a flavor of conspiracy."

"Is it treason if the lives of thousands of men are spared?" asked Mercant. "If we want to help the Chief, we can do it by avoiding any conflict that could develop into a cosmic war. Don't we need every minute possible to be able to combat Rhodan's terrible illness? On Saos we'll never find out anything about this mysterious planet Trakarat if we shoot down the Antis. Besides, Atlan wouldn't permit that."

"You win," said Bell, finally yielding. "Colonel, try to make contact with the Arkonide flagship."

Claudrin's hefty physique usually made him appear to move slowly but in this case he responded to the order with unexpected swiftness.

Bell spoke to Krefenbac. "Tell them to let us know when Rhodan has his new uniform. I don't want him to show up here just when we're in the middle of a conversation with Atlan."

In his mind he had a distressing vision of Rhodan storming in, shouting at everybody and glaring around with those smouldering eyes of his in search of the guilty ones. It caused a strange feeling to come over him. At first he could not define it but finally he knew.

It was fear!

Whether it was a fear of losing his friend completely or due to some other cause was immaterial at the moment. Only one thing was plain: his uneasiness had developed into a sense of fear. It would not be long, perhaps, before the feeling would give way to horror.

And then?

Bell closed his eyes. Suddenly he wished that he were far away from all this—away from Saos and the *Ironduke* and this whole nasty business. He longed for quiet and seclusion. He told himself it was his nerves. The constant overstrain and stress was getting to him.

He watched silently while Claudrin made the necessary connections for transmitting. He kept glancing uneasily toward the entrance hatch of the Control Central. With Rhodan's present unpredictability it was possible for him to show up at any time.

In his haste, Claudrin had completely bypassed the Communications Central. He switched on the video portion of the space-com channel. "We are in contact, sir," he announced.

Bell approached the console slowly. It was a distasteful task to have to inform Atlan in this manner. He experienced a sense of guilt when he thought of the trouble they had given the Imperator, their ancient friend who had taken over the power from the robot Brain on Arkon 3.

But it was not the Admiral's face that appeared on the screen. Bell saw an unknown Arkonide with white hair and a dark complexion.

"Gen. Toseff here," said the stranger. "What do you want, Terran?"

The voice was cold and haughty. For an Arkonide the General radiated a surprising amount of personal energy. Bell got hold of himself. Now was not the time to act offended. He had to deal with the man.

"My name is Reginald Bell," he said calmly. "Connect me with Gonozal VIII, Imperator of Arkon."

Toseff's smile seemed to be arrogant and scornful. "His Highness will only speak to the First Administrator," he retorted.

Bell took an involuntary step toward the video panel. His fists were clenched. Mercant sensed Bell's indignation in time to intervene.

"Rhodan is sick. Transmit that to the Imperator. Tell him that it's vitally necessary . . . ."

Toseff interrupted sharply. "It is useless for you to try such a ruse!"

Before Bell could tell the Arkonide that he was an inflated pipsqueak, the General disappeared from the screen and Atlan took his place. The immortal looked weary.

"Alright, Bell," he said calmly, "Gen. Toseff was only following my orders."

Bell's glowering expression did not change. "Perry does not know that we are talking to you," he explained. "All of us —Mercant, John Marshall, Freyt, Claudrin and everybody else—would like to pull the Solar Fleet out of the Arkonide Imperium. But that's not so easy. A change has come over Perry since his imprisonment on Okul. He hasn't yet gotten over the shock. Besides that he's suffering from something the doctors describe as an explosive cell-division. He keeps on growing heavier and taller. You'd hardly recognize him anymore."

"I don't get the connection," said Atlan coldly. "What has his sickness to do with Saos?"

"Perry believes the Antis are responsible for his illness. He wants to force them to help him. He figures they may be able to stop the uncontrolled expansion of his cell-growth. We are in search of a mysterious planet called Trakarat. It's supposed to be the central world of the Baalol cult. The priests tried to fool us into believing that Saos is Trakarat."

"The encroachments of the Solar Fleet are increasing," complained the Imperator. "No one can expect us to keep putting up with Rhodan's dangerous extravagances."

Mercant had tried to remain passive during this but finally had to break in again urgently: "We are Rhodan's friends, Atlan, as well as yourself. Please give us support in helping him as quickly as possible. His present condition is so serious that we must fear the worst if something isn't done soon. He issues commands and instructions that he would have considered ludicrous in the past.''

"Pull the Terran ships out of here," Atlan demanded. "There is no other alternative."

"If you could only see him!" shouted Bell heatedly. "How can you refuse to help us? Have you forgotten what he's done for you and your Imperium? Do you think all that would have been done with the intention of destroying it? No, Perry is sick, and that's why we can't condemn him for his actions. We have to capture the acting high priest of Saos. He's bound to have information that can help us further in our search."

A deep furrow formed between Atlan's brows and for a moment his hand was visible as he briefly covered his eyes. It struck Bell as astonishing how similar this man was to Perry Rhodan—the *old* Rhodan! After a period of deliberation in which the only sound was the humming of the equipment, the undying Admiral finally spoke.

"This means—that you will attack Saos?"

"Yes." Bell and Mercant answered simultaneously.

"You know, this conversation *could* be a diversionary trick on your part. Otherwise I have no recourse but to believe that you speak the truth."

"As we have many times before this," said Bell quietly. He was not inclined to contest Atlan's suspicions because if he had been in the Imperator's boots he would probably be thinking the same way. In any event it didn't hurt to remind Atlan that he had always trusted his Terran friends in the past.

"I may be committing a grave error," said Atlan, "but for the time being I'll hold back the fleet. I'll deploy all ships into a spherical formation that will enclose the Saos System. If anything happens that isn't in line with this discussion I will order an immediate attack. No Terran ship will be able to get thru the defense wall of major-class robot warships.''

For the firstime a smile appeared on Bell's face. ''There is a possibility of preventing a full-scale attack against Saos,'' he said cryptically. He noted that both Atlan and Mercant were looking at him with awakened interest but he did not feel inclined to enlighten them further. ''It's just a thought,'' he hastened to explain. ''Now everything will depend on what Perry decides to do.''

Maj. Krefenbac interrupted. ''Sir! The robots have finished the uniform. They have just delivered it to Rhodan in his cabin.''

''Let's cut this off, Admiral,'' Bell suggested. ''Let's all keep our thumbs up!'' It was a spaceman's phrase that was untranslatable yet universally understood.

Atlan slowly raised both hands showing upright thumbs but he moved them back and forth significantly. ''I only have two,'' he replied but for the firstime his voice sounded somewhat friendlier.

No one had to explain to the officers of the *Ironduke* what the Imperator was trying to tell them. It was hope mixed with pragmatic realism, as tho to say he did not foresee a very good outcome for the situation. Both sides had become too deeply committed.

Jefe Claudrin shut off the vidcom. ''We still have a chance of holding him off,'' he commented.

Everything now depended upon Rhodan. Bell couldn't help shuddering inwardly at the thought of Rhodan's return to the Control Central. A double responsibility lay on his own shoulders. He was also under obligation to Atlan.

Allan D. Mercant raised his voice slightly. "Mr. Bell, it's time to let us share your thoughts . . . "

* * * *

Thomas Cardif slipped into his uniform and zipped it up. The robot that had delivered it had already left the cabin. In secret appraisal he glanced down at himself. It seemed to him that the uniform alterations set him off to advantage. His bloated body acquired a new appearance of firmness. Without any qualms of propriety he fastened to his chest all of the medals and orders of merit that his father had rightfully been entitled to. His hands trembled in the process because he was in a hurry now.

He was firmly convinced that Atlan would talk to him and beg for peace. If necessary he could call in many more Terran ships to the Saos theater of action.

He regarded himself in what was left of the shattered mirror. A wide crack in the glass near the upper frame divided his face in halves so that his appearance was even more demonic than it was in actuality. He chuckled grimly to himself. It was time for this demon to *force* the search for his salvation.

Thus resolved, he marched stiffly from the cabin. The passage he followed was only intermittently lighted and each time he moved beyond a circle of illumination a distorted shadow leapt before him across the deck, only to be obliterated by another pool of light. He avoided using the conveyor strip, preferring to continue in this manner along the corridor, somehow fascinated by the phenomenon. Thru narrowed eyes he watched the constant jumping and fading of his shadow. A strange parallel here, he thought—like a moth leaping from flame to flame, repeatedly repelled and darting forward again . . .

Suddenly another shape appeared. The insane impression

shot thru Cardif's mind that this might be the physical embodiment of his shadow. He reached out his hands for it gropingly.

"Sir . . ." someone uttered.

It required an effort for Cardif to tear himself out of his strange fixation. He focussed his eyes sharply upon the figure of the deckwatch officer. "What's the matter?" he rasped out angrily.

The confused officer stammered: "I—I thought you weren't feeling well, sir!"

Cardif stood there like a giant bird of prey, slightly crouched forward with his hands out like talons. He saw a glimmer of fear in the other man's eyes and caught the nervous trembling of his face muscles. The officer's reaction transmitted to Cardif a sense of superiority—which saved the man from a perhaps more terrifying scene.

"Get out of my way!" commanded the Administrator. "If I don't feel well I'll go to a doctor."

"Yessir!" replied the embarrassed officer.

The man stepped to one side and pressed his back against the wall. Without giving him another glance, Cardif went past him. He knew, however, that the latter's wondering gaze followed him.

When Thomas Cardif entered the Control Central his instinct told him that something of a momentous nature had transpired here. He could not determine *what* it was but just the certainty of it served to increase his psychopathic suspicions. He forced himself to be calm as he approached the indicators. He could see that the Arkonide ships were in motion again but this time there was no attack formation.

"What's the meaning of this, Colonel?" he asked Claudrin.

"They're closing us in," explained the Epsalian. "They're forming an impenetrable blockade shell around Saos, sir. It means we can't leave the system unless Atlan permits us to.''

Cardif-Rhodan waved a hand disdainfully. "It's obvious that Atlan has cold feet," he declared, self-satisfied. "If he were so sure of himself he would have attacked by now." As he turned from Claudrin he noted Mercant's presence for the first time. "Where the devil did *you* come from?"

The security chief forced a smile. Inwardly he couldn't suppress a shudder over Rhodan's appearance. The Administrator had become a giant. "I figured you might need me here," said Mercant. "When we attack that nest of Antis down below I'll be right beside you to help."

"There are still a few valiant Terrans left, after all!" commented Cardif enthusiastically. "All I get on board the *Ironduke* is a bunch of yellow-livered yammering!"

Mercant drew himself up proudly as tho appreciative of the open compliment. Claudrin watched him grimly, reflecting that the Intelligence Chief had missed his calling—he should have been an actor.

"It's only action that brings success," said Mercant, looking about him aggressively. "But Mr. Bell and the other officers think it'll take *all* of our ships to attack such a ridiculous little Anti base . . . "

Rhodan laughed scornfully. He clapped the little man jovially on the shoulder. Mercant looked at the latter's display of medals with mixed feelings. Formerly the Administrator had always preferred a simple combat uniform. Cardif's confused mind was no longer shrewd enough to see thru the security chief's clever trap. Mercant had deliberately provoked the Administrator into a contradiction—which came immediately.

"All of our ships?" Rhodan repeated sarcastically. "I'll guarantee you we can take Saos with only 10 fighting units."

"That will allow the rest of the ships to hold off any action by

Atlan," said Mercant, and now he made no secret of his satisfaction.

With an almost indolent gesture, Cardif ended the discussion. "We attack," he ordered.

Mercant and Bell only looked at each other without saying a word. When Rhodan began to pick out the 10 ships he wanted, Reginald Bell's strategy went into effect. Lieutenants Brazo Alkher and Stana Nolinov were to be part of the attack group's top command. They were the best informed concerning the Anti stronghold.

Thomas Cardif could not know that a second group was going to land at the same time as his attack force moved in.

But everything hinged on how long Atlan would stand still. His mighty robotships surrounded Saos with a ring of steel while multi-thousands of heavy gun turrets swiveled threateningly.

10 heavy cruisers dropped away from the Terran fleet and plunged into the upper atmosphere of the planet. Their powerful retro-engines blasted thru the heavy strata of nitrogen and carbon-dioxide gases, causing the sky to tremble.

The battle for Saos had begun.

50 ADVENTURES FROM NOW
Kurt Brand tells us of
Contact Ship TERRANIA

5/   THE NEMESIS EYE

Hanoor was the oldest priest stationed on Saos. This may have been the reason he had been appointed temporary acting High Priest so that Kutlos and his deputy Tasnor could go groping around in the ruins of the power plant while Hepna-Kaloot led them into the deadliest phase of the game of Paloot.

Hanoor did not feel in any way that his new assignment was a burden. He was an old man who had seen and experienced much in his life. Inwardly he was governed by a special kind of calm. He only did whatever was absolutely necessary.

When the operators at the indicator consoles announced that the Arkonide fleet was drawing back and forming a barrier shell around the Saos System, Hanoor surmised that Gonozal VIII was going to remain as an observer for the time being. He gave the order to man all the ground defense batteries and put them in combat readiness. The underground defense installations opened their hatches and elevated the long-barreled projectors of their energy guns. Hanoor also had hand weapons issued because inevitably it would come to a matter of close combat. The old priest allowed himself no illusions about being able to stop the Terran ships before they made a landing.

With cool composure he watched the spherical Arkonide spaceships change their positions. It did not disturb him that the

Imperator had decided to go into a holding formation. His unshakable calm had its effect on the other priests as well. Willingly they followed the instructions of this ancient and bearded one in his venerable cape as he hurried from station to station to personally convince himself of the fighting morale of the Antis.

When he returned to the observation center of the great pyramid he held a short briefing session. "If Gonozal VIII does not come to our aid," he told them in his frail voice, "we will lose this battle. Nevertheless we will not surrender. Each of us is duty-bound to hold out with all the strength at our command."

He inspected his own energy weapon and took a seat in front of the panoramic viewscreens. Reports were coming to him from all sides. Every move of the spaceships was being watched.

Hanoor looked at his hands, which had long since lost their youthful vigor and tone. How old did a man have to be, he thought, before he must fight no longer? Never too old, perhaps. He wondered at the phlegmatic processes of his thoughts now. If a man became old enough he simply died and then it was over with. As a secret smile came to his face the priests sitting near him looked at him in wonderment.

Well then, he thought serenely, this was a time for dying, so let it come. In earlier days such thoughts would have disturbed him and the approach of death would have upset his inner composure completely.

Someone shouted: "Hanoor!"

It startled him out of his reveries. He knew immediately what had happened. The screens clearly revealed what was transpiring in the upper layers of the atmosphere: 10 Terran ships had separated from the fleet and were thundering toward the surface of Saos. Hanoor hunched forward in his seat and watched the viewscreen before him. His lustreless eyes were like two stones.

His ancient voice became shrill. "Attention, all defense batteries and combat stations!" he shouted. "Stand ready to fire!"

The confirmations came back immediately. The Antis behind their heavy energy guns and at the ground-to-air torpedo ramps held themselves tensely in readiness. Once again the Saos stronghold awakened to hectic activity.

Hanoor's calm challenge sounded forth from every loud-speaker: "Give them a reception they will not soon forget!"

Even Kutlos, the former acting High Priest, was able to hear this call to action. But he had no time to think about it: 50 meters ahead of him lay Tasnor and 20 meters beyond him his antagonist was waiting for him.

* * * *

Kutlos lay flat on the ground. His pulse was racing. Ahead of him where Tasnor's crumpled figure was lying a haze of dust hung in the air. Tasnor had fallen in the rubble of a wall that had failed to resist the Springers' sham attack. He was badly wounded. Hepna-Kaloot's treacherous attack had come too swiftly for the youngster. The chubby little priest had guided the monitor skillfully so that it had struck him like a lightning bolt.

Kutlos had not dared to aim a shot at the spy device for fear of hitting Tasnor, his runner. The thing had then shot away low over the ground and since then Hepna-Kaloot had remained in hiding.

The ground under Kutlos was strangely still. The stamping and rumbling of the giant manufacturing plant for producing defense screen projectors had long since been silenced. For

Kutlos the noise of the automatic installations had become a familiar part of his life on Saos. Now the disassembled feeder lines were stored in the transportships at the spaceport. The robot-controlled production centers had been rendered useless thru the sham attack of the Springers. Now it appeared that the valuable equipment in the ships' holds would not ever be salvaged or brought to safety. The Solar Fleet had gotten here much sooner than expected.

Kutlos looked about him warily. He had to keep a continuous lookout for the silent approach of the monitor eye which could give Hepna-Kaloot a clear view of his location and movements. However he could see no sign of it at the moment. The balance of weapons-strength had now gone to Hepna-Kaloot's advantage. As Kutlos' runner, Tasnor was badly wounded and out of action, while Hepna-Kaloot could still use all his weapons the same as before.

In spite of this the stocky little Anti had remained deliberately on the defensive. He had steadily retreated from Kutlos, who had no other recourse but to keep following his enemy's trail. But the brutal attack on Tasnor had changed this pattern to the extent that the retreating movement stopped because Kutlos had stopped. The treacherous innovation with the floating monitor had made him especially cautious.

What Kutlos still couldn't figure out was what Hepna-Kaloot expected to do with his cannister of water. Rack his brain tho he might he could not imagine how water could be used as a weapon. Yet his opponent had represented himself as an experienced Paloot fighter. He must certainly have a definite purpose in mind in choosing the cannister because he had seemed so sure that he could overcome Kutlos with it.

Still gripping his raygun, Kutlos remained hidden behind his cover. He was thinking of the order he had heard Hanoor issue over the P.A. system. The Terrans evidently were not giving up their invasion plan. Which was a good thing in one sense, thought Kutlos, because it would serve to goad the Imperator into action.

His train of thought was interrupted by a groan from Tasnor.

He didn't want to risk calling out any words of encouragement to him for fear of betraying his own location. Kutlos did not exclude the possibility that Hepna-Kaloot knew where he was but was playing it safe for the moment. The dust raised by Tasnor's fall by the ruined wall had begun to settle again. It deposited a gray coating over the young priest's remaining clothing. Kutlos belly-crawled around 2 larger segments of shattered masonry, which made him conscious again of the impractical cape he still wore. Yet he still hesitated to remove this symbol of his dignity and station.

Then he saw the spying eye!

All this time it had been in his immediate vicinity. Instead of being overhead where he had expected it to appear, it was *ahead* of him between 2 broken wall segments. Thru the narrow cleft the insidious device gleamed like a smouldering ember —balefully. It was by pure chance that he had discovered it. So Hepna-Kaloot knew exactly where the high priest was located and what he was doing. Kutlos was grudgingly forced to admire the skillful manner in which the TV eye was being utilized.

By a conscious act of will he suppressed his initial reaction to fire at the robot spy. Undoubtedly Hepna-Kaloot was watching him like a cat and at his first suspicious movement he would make the thing flit out of range.

The high priest avoided looking directly at the hiding place of the monitor. He knew he mustn't let on that he had seen it. He lay there in tense perplexity, realizing that he'd probably have only a single chance to strike a counterblow. The main thing was to be very clever about it. A quick shot was out of the question as Hepna-Kaloot would react instantly and besides the flying camera was well protected behind its barrier.

He bit his lower lip, tensing for new action. Turning on his side he glanced unobtrusively toward the glowering eye. And then an idea came to him. Carefully and calmly he began to unwind the Lagoo rope. He had to make it appear to Hepna-Kaloot that he merely wanted to examine the line. As the elastic material slipped thru his hands it seemed to be like a snake—and in a certain sense a Lagoo rope was designed to operate like a reptile. Generally the priests used it for binding prisoners. The cord had a spontaneous reflex of its own. Once it was set in motion toward an opponent the latter was usually powerless to escape from it.

Initially Kutlos had intended to use the rope while in close combat with Hepna-Kaloot but now his plan was changed. He would use it against the other priest's most dangerous weapon.

Against the nemesis eye!

* * * *

He could feel his pulse pounding harder now and the rush of blood brought a flush of heat to his scalp. Hepna-Kaloot had placed his micro-screen in front of him and was intently observing the high priest's movements as well as everything in the surrounding area.

The robot spy had 3 "eyes", any of which the operator could switch on at his option. The frontal orb was flanked by 2 auxiliary eyes. In its present position the frontal eye was sufficient since it was the only one that could give a direct line of sight toward Kutlos' hiding place between the masonry fragments.

Hepna-Kaloot was gratified to notice his opponent's increasing nervousness. Kutlos kept looking above him and fumbling around with his Lagoo rope. Tasnor was already knocked out of the combat. Hepna-Kaloot practically caressed the water cannister and his Sostoos knife. Before he died in the attack bombardment of the Terrans he wanted to prove to himself and the high priest that he—the insignificant little man with no influence or apparent importance—was the stronger of the two after all.

He knew that Kutlos couldn't hold out much longer in his

present position. Soon he would attempt to leave his cover and come hunting for him—and that would be the end of him.

A dark shadow flitted across the viewscreen. It happened so suddenly that Hepna-Kaloot needed a second or so to collect his wits. The picture fluttered, became blurred and then vanished. He shouted a curse and shook the micro-receiver. But in the next moment he froze, gripped by a sudden realization.

"By Holy Baalol!" he exclaimed to himself. "He's released the Lagoo rope against the monitor!"

Apparently one of the rope's multiple tendrils had wrapped itself around the frontal lens of the viewer and was trying to draw the device upward into the line of fire of Kutlos' raygun. Hepna-Kaloot went into frenzied action. He spun the main rheostat of the control box around to its limit so that all energy reserves of the monitor would be turned on. The raster of the micro-screen flickered uncertainly, alternately producing a pattern of lines and an intermittent picture of the high priest's grimly determined features.

Hepna-Kaloot switched on one of the lateral "eyes" of the remote device. From what he could determine there were now 2 arms of the rope which had wrapped themselves around the monitor. One of them was directly over the frontal lens, blurring his reception, and thru the lateral lens Kutlos could not be seen.

He switched the remote power to full and drew the monitor back, low over the ground. The ropy tendrils were dragged along a short distance before they could anchor themselves on some chunks of fallen masonry. This happened within 5 meters of Kutlos' hiding place. Hepna-Kaloot activated the other auxiliary lens and saw to his horror that another rope strand was taking hold of the flying instrument. He knew he could not keep the driving force of the device going at maximum power because it would soon drain the batteries. Quickly he manipulated his control switches and the robot spy dropped toward the ground. The Lagoo strands coiled like rubber and dragged the stone anchorages with them. There was a recoil action which banged the monitor against the earth.

Hepna-Kaloot threw in a new burst of maximum power and drove the box at full speed toward Kutlos' location. This freed the camera eye and it raced onward. He cried out in triumph but in that moment one of the Lagoo tendrils whipped out from behind and attached itself to one of the side lenses. The rest of the rope coils rolled after it with a feathery lightness while Hepna-Kaloot glowered at the picture transmitted by the forward lens. Kutlos couldn't be seen from this angle anymore but he was no doubt waiting for a chance to take a shot at the monitor.

Now the rope strands swept over the box like so many tentacles. He shut down the power because at the moment an attempt to break away would have been useless. He had made poor use of his chance to free the robot viewer. Instead of getting it up into the clear he had only brought it more completely into the rope's range of action.

But it was useless to brood about the mistake at this stage. He alternately switched on one lens of the box after another but none of them offered a clear picture transmission. The Lagoo rope had ensnared the monitor entirely. In fact it was slowly raising the device into the air—a process which he knew would continue until Kutlos could get a clear shot at it.

At that moment, however, would be the time to take swift action. If Kutlos didn't want to risk destroying the rope, which was one of his weapons, he would have to wait until the strands had let go. In that fraction of a second while the spy box hung free in the air, everything would depend upon who was the quickest to act: Hepna-Kaloot at his remote controls or Kutlos with his trigger finger.

The two Antis were so engrossed in their own battle that they were not aware of the approaching 10 cruisers of the Solar Fleet until one of the other energy plants went up in a mighty explosion.

100 ADVENTURES FROM NOW
H.G. Ewers takes us to
Terror Terminus

6/ TRACKING DOWN TRAKARAT

The explosive eruption of dust, torn earth, molten pieces of metal and plastic, flaming wood fragments and bubbling globules of incandescent glass was only discernible as an energy burst on the sensor indicator of the Korvette space-jet.

"It's started!" exclaimed Lt. Stant Nolinov as he switched on the propulsion system of the small craft. The ponderous airlock hatches of the hangar had opened and the rush of air into the outer void created enough suction to ripple the rubber flange guides on the doors.

Bell's freckled face appeared on the vidcom screen. "You know what's at stake for us in this action," he said gravely. "Take no unnecessary chances. Our 10 ships have met with heavy defense fire. The fight can't last another hour. You know what you have to do."

"You can count on us, sir," answered Nolinov, and Alkher added a confirming, "Roger, sir!"

"One of the round dome structures has just been wiped out," Bell reported.

"That has to be one of the Antis' four power stations," commented Alkher. "We detected the explosion on the sensor."

"Take off now," Bell ordered. "And good luck!"

The viewscreen went blank. The Korvette, long nicknamed "Guppy" by the Solar Fleet, was designated simply as the F-32. Now it swept out of the hangar and shot into space in the vicinity of Saos. On board was a 32-man team which was operating under special orders of Reginald Bell and Allan D. Mercant. The combat commandoes were equipped with a new kind of special weapon. It was a combination impulse beamer and automatic rifle. The double-barreled hand-gun simultaneously fired a thermo-beam along with a stream of antimagnetic plastic bullets. The normal projectiles were released a fraction of a second later than the light-speed energy beam so that both types of shots would reach the target together.

It was thus a weapon that was effective no matter what the enemy did. If the Antis were using the mental phase of their defense screen the plastic bullets would get thru. If they switched to normal screening the heat ray would get thru. It wasn't possible for the Antis to switch back and forth fast enough to avoid destruction in one form or another.

The task assignment had been clearly outlined for the 2 lieutenants. They were to work swiftly under cover of the general attack of the 10 ships led by the Administrator. As a result of their previous imprisonment on Saos, Nolinov and Alkher were most familiar with the terrain. Their objective was to capture the acting high priest of the Anti stronghold. By means of interrogating this important man, Bell and Mercant hoped to obtain vital data concerning the mystery-shrouded planet Trakarat which was supposed to be the homeworld of the Baalol sect.

Bell and Mercant doubted that Cardif's 10-ship attack against the base would be successful. This is why they had placed the Guppy at the disposal of the 2 lieutenants. Thirty determined men accompanied by 2 officers who had begun their main careers on board the linear-drive spaceship *Fantasy*. There were no mutants in this group since it would have been useless to use them against the paranormal capabilities of the Antis.

Stant Nolinov flew the small craft in wide circles as he

spiraled down into the planet's atmosphere. The guppy was not going to land. All hands wore the Arkonide combat suits which would enable them to make a high-altitude jump. Also the suits' deflectors could provide them with almost complete invisibility. In other words the complex screening kept the commandoes from reflecting any light. Everywhere in the universe normal optical vision depended upon light reflections, which the brain reassembled into the corresponding objects out of a confused pattern of impressions.

The ship's autopilot would guide it back to the hangar of the *Ironduke* and at any time it was needed it could be resummoned by means of radio.

Brazo Alkher was watching the tracking indicator. "The Antis don't seem to be thinking of any capitulation," he said.

"Maybe they're still hoping that Atlan will come to their aid," commented Nolinov. His crewcut hair took on a golden sheen in the reflection of the indicator lights.

Alkher scratched the back of his head thoughtfully. "It would be best to make our jump in the area of the spaceport," he suggested. "The main heat of the battle should be around the pyramid and the power stations."

"Don't you think, sir, that those transport ships will be guarded?" This question came from Jeremy Mitchum, a young man with amazingly long arms.

"That's more than possible," admitted Alkher, "but we have the advantage of surprise. Don't forget that the Antis are only going to know we're there when our 2-way shooters are under their noses." Their special double-barreled weapons had already received this nickname from Bell altho he personally preferred "double persuaders".

Mitchum pretended to aim an imaginary "persuader". Not finding a suitable opponent he stretched his arms out toward a companion, who drew back in mock horror. It was something to

see whenever Mitchum really extended his arms. In his home-
land in South America it was said of him that he could shake
hands with somebody clear across the Amazon.

"Alright, Mitchum, hold it down," Alkher told him, grin-
ning. "You'll have plenty of chance to be an eager beaver when
we get there."

Nolinov still held the Guppy in its spiral descent pattern but
Alkher was keeping a close eye on the indicators and he finally
raised a hand.

"That's low enough, Stant."

Nolinov switched over to automatic and allowed the ship to
hover on its antigravs.

Alkher spoke to Bell over the microphone. "We're bailing
out, sir!"

Bell's voice returned over the audio: "OK, Lieutenant—we'll
be hauling in the F-32 on the guidance beam."

Brazo hooked his double-barreled weapon to the utility belt
on his combat suit. "We'll jump at intervals of 3 seconds
each," he ordered. "Don't forget to switch on your deflectors.
As soon as we land we'll make ourselves visible and start the
attack. If the spaceport is unguarded we'll fly immediately to the
central base. By that time the landing units from the ships will
have shown up there."

The 32 men lined up facing the airlock. Alkher was in the
lead, suddenly silhouetted against the dreary-looking sky as the
outer hatch opened. He turned on his antigrav, nodded once to
Nolinov and disappeared.

"After him!" shouted Nolinov hoarsely over his helmet
phone.

When he made his jump he saw a distant lightning bolt which
was caused by a tremendous explosion. It was followed by a
delayed roll of thunder.

"That was Power Station #2, Stant!" called Alkher.

Nolinov spread out his arms altho it was not necessary. The antigrav system sustained him easily as he floated downward. When he turned his head to look back he saw only the receding F-32 because the commando troops were invisible. The sounds of battle increased. The sustained thunder overriding the hissing and roaring of energy weapons came from the impulse engines of the invading cruisers.

Nolinov shook his head involuntarily. He could not understand why Rhodan was actually attempting a landing here. Why didn't he hold them above the base and have his men descend as he and the special commandoes were doing? As it turned out later only two of the cruisers made a landing and that was only because the ground fire had put them out of commission.

Alkher, still in the lead, saw the flat area of the spaceport appear beyond the shoulders of the mountains. The ships of the Antis seemed to be so many toys lying there below on the field, being forced to await their fate while the Antis continued to put up a stubborn resistance.

Alkher was first to land and he shut off his deflector. He had set himself down between two of the transportships, where no Antis were in evidence. One after another the other men appeared in quick succession around him. Nolinov was the last to appear but his short and stocky figure continued in motion. He ran across the plastic steel landing pad to the bow of the nearest Baalol ship and then rose up on his antigrav to survey the entire area.

"It's a ghost town here," he reported to Alkher. "They've concentrated their total defense at the center of the base."

Alkher smiled grimly. "Let's give Mitchum a chance to let off some of that steam! Deflectors on again—we fly to the pyramid!"

They lifted up invisibly from the smooth surface of the spaceport and floated away toward the center of the conflict.

* * * *

The shockwave of the second explosion was so powerful that Kutlos thought his lungs would collapse. He gasped for air and threw himself onto the ground on his back. There was an audible sound like heavy hail as the particles of debris rained down from the sky. He finally raised up on his elbows and tried to see thru the swirling clouds of dust.

Hepna-Kaloot's spy monitor lay shattered near Tasnor's body. The Lagoo rope was nowhere to be seen. The high priest was seized by a violent fit of coughing.

The Terrans were attacking in spite of the hovering presence of the Arkonide fleet, from which Kutlos had expected assistance. He began to realize his error in having permitted Hepna-Kaloot to draw him into this game of death. In spite of the threat of an alien invasion he had been distracted by this private matter and had answered the other priest's impudent challenge. He was more horrified by his dereliction of duty than he was by the attack of the Terrans. He knew he had to return immediately to the temple's control room in order to lead the defense.

He arose and stood there, swaying for a moment between the ruins of the wall until a grating sound made him turn. A figure staggered out of the pall of dust. "Hepna-Kaloot!" shouted Kutlos. "The Solar Fleet is attacking!"

The little priest still carried the water cannister altho it had burst open on one side and had lost much of its contents. Kutlos decided to ignore him and turned away down a nearby passage. Everywhere he had to clamber over rubble and destruction. He could tell by the repeated whistling sounds that the defense batteries had gotten the ground-to-air missiles into action. Up in Control Central somebody must have taken command in time. He breathed a sigh of relief. Perhaps there was still something that could be saved.

A group of heavily-armed priests was running toward him.

"This way!" he shouted. "Follow me! We must go to the spaceport!"

They did not appear to recognize him because they came to a stop and warily raised their weapons. Kutlos looked down at himself and realized he was covered with dust and dirt and his clothing was in shreds.

"It's the High Priest!" yelled one of the Antis.

Kutlos passed his palm over his face and it felt as tho it were covered with a layer of fuzz and scum. He looked thru one of the nearby windows just as one of the low-roofed buildings exploded. The entire roof soared upward and was engulfed in clouds of burning gases and smoke while the supporting walls sagged inward, broke asunder and dissolved into rubble and dust.

"To the spaceport!" he shouted again.

Acrid smoke was coming in from all sides and farther ahead a gray-black cloud of it was pouring thru a break in the wall, threatening to obscure their vision entirely. Thru the general bedlam came Hanoor's voice over the loudspeakers but Kutlos couldn't understand what the old priest was saying.

The armed group of Antis joined him and he ran ahead of them, leading the way. Someone behind him reached a weapon to him. The weight of the heavy metal against his hip was reassuring. The men were coughing and gasping and the smoke brought tears to their eyes as they stumbled over fallen beams and great chunks of masonry. They came to the place that had served as cover to Kutlos during his contest with Hepna-Kaloot. The belligerent little priest was nowhere to be seen but Tasnor was still there. He had sat up finally and was looking about him in wide-eyed perplexity, muttering incoherently to himself. Kutlos came to the younger man's side and bent over him to see his condition. Tasnor's gaze was blank and lustreless, being focussed on what Kutlos silently presumed to be the realm of death.

"Go away!" Tasnor mumbled. There was neither hate nor anger in his voice—only rejection and an infinite yearning for peace. Kutlos placed both arms around the youngster to support him.

"You have to get out of here!" he said gently. "The Terrans are attacking the station in their ships."

For a moment it seemed to him that he might succeed in pulling the priest back to the present. There was a momentary flicker of life in the staring eyes but it was only an unconscious reaction. Tasnor's will was not behind it. Kutlos let him sink back gently.

He straightened up and turned to the others. "Let's continue," he said tonelessly.

They moved around Tasnor's body without looking at him and hurried their steps to escape the sight of their dying companion.

The main force of the Terran attack was being concentrated on the central station, of that Kutlos was certain. He had also noted that a relatively small number of ships were engaged in the action. This could mean that the main forces of the Solar Fleet were in a space battle with the robot flotillas of the Imperator. For Kutlos it was a reassuring thought altho he had no facts to substantiate it.

His deliberations were interrupted when a number of men

penetrated the passageway thru a nearby hole in the wall. In the dust and smoke it was difficult to recognize who they were but in any case they were a welcome reinforcement to his group.

Then Kutlos came to a stop. These were no servants of Baalol nor were they the hoped-for Arkonides. They were Terrans!

Out of pure instinct the high priest turned on his individual defense screen and opened fire.

* * * *

They landed in the area of the third power station and Brazo Alkher shut off his deflector. Nolinov emerged out of invisibility near him. He was streaming sweat but he grinned.

"Familiar territory!" Brazo called to him, referring to their imprisonment here.

He looked around him warily. Cardif had not yet landed with troops but the Antis' defensive fire had already grown weaker.

A commando named Buster Coleman came up to him. "Over there, sir!" he said. "The walls have fallen in and we can enter without having to blast an opening."

"Mitchum!" Alkher called out.

The man from Brazil appeared at his side and looked at him expectantly.

"Take 3 men and check that broken wall. If things are clear inside we'll use it as our entrance."

"Yessir!" Mitchum picked out 3 men and started out.

Alkher watched as the four of them ran toward the building with the double persuaders in their hands. They clambered over fallen rubble and Mitchum was the first to duck inside the structure. Immediately he reappeared and signaled with his long arms, as if to say "All clear." In that same moment a small ammunition depot blew up under the impact of an impulse beam.

"No danger at all," commented Nolinov drily. Apparently there was more danger of being hit by their own ships than there was of being caught in Anti counterfire.

Alkher lifted his weapon arm. "Let's go!" he shouted.

Mitchum's lanky figure was discolored by smoke and half covered with dust when they reached him.

"Everything's in order, sir," reported the South American. He jerked a thumb over his shoulder. "Inside—it's all clear."

They squeezed thru the opening in the shattered wall and entered a smoke-filled corridor in which nothing could be seen beyond a distance of 20 meters or so.

"Sir, I'd say we'd better—"

Whatever Mitchum was going to say remained unfinished. Alkher was shocked to see the Brazilian raise his hands in the air, after which he collapsed silently to the ground. In front of them, vague figures in waving capes were emerging out of the opaque clouds of smoke.

"Antis!" yelled Nolinov.

Alkher reacted almost instinctively. In one jump he was behind a shoulder of the broken wall, where he readied his weapon. Somebody cried out in sudden pain and then the passage was filled with the roaring and hissing bedlam of combat fire. Alkher felt a painful knot in his stomach when he saw 4 dead Terran commandoes who had not gotten out of the way in time. Biting his lip in a mixture of rage and anguish, he moved into the battle and opened fire.

A strange thought came to him in the midst of it. He was thinking that while he was here fighting for his life there were countless young men like himself back on Earth who were pleasantly pursuing more peaceful occupations without the slightest awareness of a certain Lt. Brazo Alkher. By his presence here, along with the crews of the Solar Fleet, he was helping to guarantee that men of Earth and all humans on far colonial planets would be able to live in peace.

* * * *

The firstime Kutlos was hit he knew that he would never reach the transportships alive. Against the special weapons of the invaders his individual screen was not enough to protect him any longer. He lay motionlessly behind a shattered switch cabinet and pressed his face against the cool surface of the metal. One after the other they would end like this. Gonozal VIII had abandoned them. The plan of Holy Baalol had failed.

Someone close to him groaned. Kutlos started to move away from the cabinet while waves of pain raged thru his body. He peered across a burst jumble of wires, coils and shattered tubes. Before he could see his wounded companion he was hit again. This time there wasn't much to feel except that the strength ebbed swiftly from his legs.

The unknown wounded man groaned again. Kutlos grasped 2 protruding fuse boxes and drew himself over the polished surface of the fallen cabinet. He slipped over the other side of it onto the floor. He saw no one. A strange sensation pervaded the lower part of his body and it almost seemed as if his legs were made of wax. He ran his hands over his body and when he brought them back they were smeared with blood. He began to wonder why nobody around him was putting up any resistance against the Terrans.

"They've run away," he muttered to himself bitterly. But then he noticed that the sound of fighting in the passage had ceased entirely.

Footsteps approached him. Kutlos strained with all his might to get up but nothing happened. It cost him such an effort that he had to close his eyes in complete exhaustion. Somebody pulled the blasted switch cabinet away and the screeching of metal seemed to him to be excruciatingly loud.

He opened his eyes and saw a row of combat boots. When he elevated his gaze he saw the owners of the boots and finally their faces looking down at him from high above as thru a mist: Terrans. One of the faces came nearer to him, lean and angular with earnest brown eyes. Somehow this man seemed to be familiar—and then he remembered: he was one of the prisoners they had allowed to escape during the sham battle with the Springers.

"Kutlos!" the Terran called out to him.

"I hear you," he answered with dignity, speaking in Interkosmo. "Whatever it is you want from me you must hurry—*Tav dordo* . . . I am dying."

Brazo Alkher swiftly inspected the high priest and saw that he was wounded in 2 places. He frowned while struggling with mixed feelings. Young Mitchum lay behind him already dead.

"Kutlos—is the planet Trakarat the central world of the Baalol cult?" he asked.

Kutlos only nodded since speech was difficult for him now.

Alkher interrogated swiftly. "Can you give us the position data for Trakarat or any other information on it?"

"I could," said Kutlos with an effort.

"Then speak!" demanded the Terran.

"No." It was a flat denial but quite simple since he could speak no more. Knowing that death was claiming him now he either remained silent in response to each question or laughed in scorn.

Shortly after that his head sank back and his eyes stared lifelessly. Brazo Alkher straightened up resignedly and seemed to swallow with difficulty.

"No use," he said with a note of despair in his voice. "It was all for nothing."

* * * *

The Baalol defense lines gradually collapsed and Cardif's attack rolled onward in full force against the last pockets of resistance. The special commando team under Alkher and Nolinov pulled back to the spaceport. The 2 lieutenants did not have much to say to each other. Behind them in the ruins lay five of their men for whom nothing more could be done. They had brought 2 more with them who were gravely wounded. The men were in a dejected mood since the price had been high for little or no information concerning Trakarat.

"Maybe Rhodan has had more luck than we did," said Nolinov finally.

Alkher remained skeptical. "The Antis fought in sheer desperation and those 10 cruisers weren't exactly out to spare anybody—if there are any enemy survivors at all."

"Sir!" exclaimed somebody suddenly. It was Coleman.

Brazo turned to see what he was pointing at. Two figures were running straight across the open area. Altho they were not wearing the clothing of Anti priests they were obviously not Terrans. Apparently the 2 men were fleeing and their goal was the spaceport.

"After them!" he ordered.

He picked out 4 men, who switched on their antigravs and flew toward the fugitives.

Nolinov watched them pensively. "Somehow those two seem to look familiar to me," he said.

"That's impossible," Alkher told him. "How could you know them?"

Nolinov didn't seem to want to express his suspicion. He

remained silent as they continued their march toward the transport ships. On account of the wounded, whose suits were damaged, they had refrained from using their antigravs. Within 10 minutes they overtook the other 4 commandoes, who had meanwhile captured the strangers. They were big, burly and savage-looking, their eyes wild with fear. One of them looked at Alkher and Nolinov with an incredulous expression on his face.

"I was right!" exclaimed Nolinov triumphantly and as Alkher looked at him uncomprehendingly he smiled and pointed to the 2 prisoners. "Old friends of ours, Brazo," he said sarcastically. "But the lastime we saw them they were supposed to be badly wounded."

"The Springers!" murmured Alkher.

It all came back to him now in vivid detail. He and Nolinov had been permitted to escape from the Antis as a part of the Baalol plan and in the process they had run into these 2 men. The priests had deliberately drawn the two Terrans to take cover on a plateau, which was the planned landing area of the Springer space lifeboat. It had been made to look like an emergency landing but naturally these two Springers had not actually been wounded. It had all been part of the sham attack for the benefit of the two Terrans. Apparently these two had not been able to return to the long-ships of their clan. Instead they had been caught here in a real attack which had led to the defeat of their allies.

Alkher stepped up to one of the Springers and clapped him roughly on the shoulder. "What happened to your injuries?" he asked ironically. "Didn't you heal up rather quickly?"

"We are peaceful Traders," the man replied. "We haven't anything to do with this situation."

His companion nodded urgently in confirmation. Alkher regarded the statement with skepticism since he knew that Galactic Traders only demonstrated their peace-loving natures when their lives were threatened. Otherwise they were not squeamish about committing any deed of violence.

"You don't say!" exclaimed Nolinov in mock astonishment. He joined his companion and aimed the persuader at the captives. "Alright," he said with sudden sharpness, "let's see how peaceful you *really* are if you're such innocent little lambs!"

Anyone who didn't know Nolinov would have been frightened of him at this moment. His eyes flashed dangerously and his face muscles hardened menacingly. It startled the two Springers, who were already intimidated. They thought despairingly of their chances for escape.

"We'll tell you anything we know," said one of the Traders quickly.

"We're searching for a specific planet," said Alkher. "It is supposed to be the central world of the Baalol cult. It is called Trakarat. What do you know about it?"

The first Springer who had spoken looked uneasily at Nolinov's double-barreled weapon before answering. "We've heard that the priests often talk about this planet. We don't know its location but it must be easy to identify because of its unusual appearance."

"What's that supposed to mean?" urged Nolinov.

"Trakarat has a double ring around it," the Springer reported, "something like one of your own planets in the Sol System. I think you call that one Saturn."

The Trader hesitated but when Alkher nodded to him he continued. "Trakarat's in a family of 15 other planets that circle a red binary star. The name of the binary is Aptut. Judging from the conversations of the priests it must be close to the center of the galaxy."

The 2 lieutenants exchanged glances. Nolinov lowered his weapon, much to the obvious relief of the two Springers.

Alkher spoke to them. "You'll be held captive until we've determined the truth of what you've told us. If you've told us lies you'll simply have to face the alternative—tell us the truth or else!"

Inwardly, however, he was already convinced of the validity of their information. The Traders were much too frightened to risk angering the Terrans with fictitious data. He turned to Nolinov. "Let's contact the *Ironduke*. Bell and Mercant may be glad to hear about this. At least we've picked up some pretty good clues and a system like Aptut's should be pretty identifiable."

"They'd better send us the guppy now," said Nolinov. "Our mission on Saos has been completed."

He activated his micro-transmitter. They were already beyond the area that had been receiving the brunt of the cruisers' annihilating bombardments. It would be only a matter of minutes before the last Anti resistance was broken and then Rhodan would be making his ground invasion of the station's ruins.

200 ADVENTURES FROM NOW
You'll
Cruise thru Magellan

7/ COSMIC DETENTE

He clambered over mountains of debris, staggered onward between caved-in sections of the walls, charged across small open areas and pressed thru choked or half-fallen doorways. He had long since ceased looking back to see if the troops were still following him. There was a constant ringing in his ears that seemed to drown out all other sounds. In the eerie twilight dimness of the shattered pyramid he came upon a maze of passages, ruptured lift-shafts and staircases that had been blasted to fragments.

Thomas Cardif felt a piercing pain in the area of his heart and had to come to a stop. Sweat covered his body, ran down between his eyebrows and stung his eyes. Suddenly he sensed the presence of men around him and as he turned around fiercely he saw them standing there—the space infantry of the Solar Fleet. They had gathered behind him shoulder to shoulder, grim-faced, silent, holding their double-barreled persuaders in readiness.

For the firstime Cardif sensed what it would feel like to *really* be Perry Rhodan. These men were following him into a battle which they considered to be senseless but they were at his side for the concept, legend or symbol that Rhodan represented to them.

He lowered his weapon and stared thru them or beyond them with a salty taste in his mouth, thinking desperately of his physical condition and his need for a cure, whether from the Antis or any other source. No matter how much he had stormed and raved at the doctors in Terrania over the space hypercom their findings had been of little consolation to him. Of course the top specialists were working day and night on the problem but no remedy was able to arrest the disastrous effects of the cell activator. As far as an operation was concerned they had told him repeatedly that such a procedure would be fatal.

"Sir!" said one of the men.

Cardif focussed his gaze on an older man with a small moustache and large gray eyes. As the soldier came up to him he recognized Sgt. Mulford, who was pointing to the heaps of debris.

"We have to try getting farther upstairs in the pyramid," said the sergeant. "I suggest we send some men up the shafts in combat suits, using their antigravs, so they can check the place out."

"The Sergeant is right, sir," agreed Lt. Yakinawo. "We can't get any farther this way."

There was no logical reason to object to such a plan yet Cardif did so: "I differ with you there," he said. "The men could be taken by surprise in the shafts. You don't know where the priests may still have nests of resistance. So we'll get upstairs the way we're going."

Yakinawo looked at him in amazement but remained silent. Cardif continued onward sullenly. Mulford's idea was the correct one, he knew, and he would have been glad to go along with it if he himself could have accompanied the men. But nowhere was there a combat suit to be found that would fit him. So he had ordered them to continue in the normal manner because he wanted to be present in case they discovered any Antis. His distrust of everyone around him had grown to the point where he would not relinquish the leadership to any subordinate officer.

"We could try this staircase here, sir," suggested Mulford

matter-of-factly and he pointed out a jumble of fallen masonry and tangled conduits and wire nearby where some stairs were visible.

Cardif looked at the sergeant speculatively. "Alright, Mulford," he said finally, "you lead the way."

Mulford was an old veteran who usually took everything in stride but in this case his big eyes widened incredulously. "You mean—you want *me* to climb up there, sir?"

"It's your suggestion," Cardif barked at him sharply. "What's the matter, do you have cold feet or something, Sergeant?"

Mulford drew up stiffly. "No sir!" he answered grimly.

He slung his persuader over his shoulder and marched toward the remains of the staircase. Without hesitation he grasped a sprung reinforcement rod and pulled himself up into the mess. Stones and rubble lying on the twisted stairs fell behind him onto the floor. The entire stair frame of partially-melted light metal begain to sway. The sergeant seemed to be a giant insect on a large seesaw which gently rocked him back and forth.

"Looks like it's holding, sir!" he called back. "I think you can follow me."

Smart alec!—thought Cardif angrily. Trying to rub it in and call my shots, is he? Does he think I'm yellow?

He climbed after Mulford and Yakinawo followed close behind him.

"Careful, sir!" Mulford's voice rang out from an uncertain elevation. "From here on it's dangerous."

Cardif looked up ahead. In one place the staircase was completely blasted to shreds and consisted practically of only 2 mangled support beams which spread out sharp twisted splinters in all directions. Mulford was like a gymnast or perhaps more like a squirrel, it seemed, as he wriggled his way on upward.

The other men were coming up the stair frame now, almost hand over hand, which swayed dangerously and seemed to bend under their weight to the accompaniment of alarming grinding noises. Cardif began to wish that he had agreed with Mulford's first suggestion. This side of the pyramid had been ripped open by a powerful explosion, exposing them to the outside. Its collapse had completely crushed one of the adjacent side buildings. Cardif didn't dare to look below him.

''Far as she goes, sir!'' called Mulford with relief. ''This is the last level. There were more above it but our ships' fire has leveled the place to here." From a safe landing platform he grinned and looked down at Cardif, who was ponderously clambering toward him.

"Can you see anybody?" asked the Administrator.

Mulford looked around behind him. "Hard to tell, sir. Place is pretty badly wrecked. There's a stink of burned wiring and cables. Looks like there was a lot of equipment up here."

Mulford's crude manner of expression was beginning to get on Cardif's nerves. However he forced himself to hold his temper because there were more important things to worry about now than putting a soldier in his place.

"Can you make it, sir?" echoed Yakinawo's worried voice behind him.

He didn't answer him as he kept on climbing. Finally Mulford was able to give him a hand and soon he was standing beside the old soldier. They turned to help Yakinawo and the other men.

"I don't think we should let so many troops come up here, sir," suggested Yakinawo. "It looks pretty dilapidated."

Cardif nodded and the Japanese officer shouted instructions into the depths. His voice echoed away into the shafts and passageways below. Cardif looked about him. At first he gathered the same impression of dust-covered debris and chaotic destruction.

Then he saw the Anti—a dark figure against a dark background who sat motionlessly in the remains of a control chair and stared at him. Cardif grasped Yakinawo's arm. The lieutenant nodded. Together with Mulford they approached the priest who sat there as tho petrified. The Baalol servant was old, one of the oldest Cardif had ever seen. The ancient one was still alive, his colorless eyes shifting restlessly from Cardif to the lieutenant.

Suddenly Cardif guessed the reason for it and he raised his

weapon. The priest knew exactly who he was. If the Anti were to betray him now, everything would be out in the open. But the old man remained silent. Cardif had been on the verge of shooting him but he finally lowered his persuader. His desperation and state of confusion were so great now that he would have fired at the oldster without compunction.

"Where can we find the High Priest?" Cardif demanded harshly.

Hanoor looked at him without expression. "Who can say?" His voice was so feeble that Cardif had to lean forward to hear him. "The realm of death is far and wide. Kutlos can be anywhere."

"Are any of his deputy high priests still alive?"

"Yes," said Hanoor, "I!"

"I have to know the location of Trakarat, old man," Cardif told him. "Tell us that and you will be free."

"Freedom," said the Anti thoughtfully, "is an ambiguous term. What form of non-freedom should an old man like me have to fear?"

Cardif was at the limit of his self-control. "The location!" he shouted. "Out with it!"

"I am weary," said Hanoor faintly. "Do not torment me."

Cardif was about to attack the helpless old man but the voice of the Japanese lieutenant deterred him. "Sir—he's not going to talk."

Hanoor closed his eyes and leaned back against the bursted headrest of the chair. He folded his thin arms over his wasted chest and his face remained as expressionless as stone. Cardif knew he would not learn the planet's position from this one —nor from any other Anti who might be found here in these ruins.

He had raised his hand to force another point but dropped it as tho he had lost his strength. Without another word he shoved his way between Mulford and Yakinawo and returned to the staircase. The Japanese lieutenant watched him go, gathering the impression of a man who was lost.

* * * *

With a concluding wave of his hand Lt. Brazo Alkher finished his report. "And that was all we could learn from the Springers, sir," he said.

The two lieutenants had returned to the Control Central of the *Ironduke* and had related their adventure to Bell, Mercant and the other officers.

Allan D. Mercant scratched his chin reflectively. "At least it's something," he said slowly, "but we can't do very much with it. There is a possibility, however, that the robot Brain on Arkon 3 might be able to do more with such information."

This brought a worried frown to Bell's face. "That would mean we'd have to get Atlan's cooperation. With the way things are at the moment he won't be in a very friendly mood—altho he did hold back his robot fleet."

Claudrin broke into the discussion. "I think it's our duty to inform the Arkonide concerning the success of the commando mission since it was only his holding still that made it possible."

"Alright, Jefe," Mercant agreed. "Set up a contact with Atlan." On the Arkonide flagship Gen. Alter Toseff had watched events on his viewscreens with a burning intentness, expecting that Gonozal VIII would order an attack. But the Imperator had merely sat there silently observing while deep in thought. Toseff had not dared to disturb the immortal in his deliberations yet he was filled with resentment against the Terrans who had attacked a planet of the Greater Imperium under the very guns of an Arkonide fleet.

If Gen. Toseff had suspected that Atlan was wishing his former allies luck, so that they could help Perry Rhodan, his rancor would have known no bounds.

The buzzing of the vidcom panel broke into Toseff's brooding train of thought. He switched on the receiver in order to take the call and in that moment the Imperator stirred out of his inactivity. He got up and came to his side. "Take it easy, General," he said.

Reginald Bell's broad face came into view. Behind him were Allan D. Mercant and that splendid fellow Claudrin, the commander of the *Ironduke*. Atlan simply could not suppress his feelings of sympathy for these men. "Well?" he inquired succinctly.

Bell looked at him uncertainly and cleared his throat noisily. "Perry has shot the blazes out of the base on Saos," he blurted out, his tone of voice making it clear that he did not approve of the action. "He'll soon be back on board without the information he was after. But my own plan worked out a little better. Lts. Alkher and Nolinov have captured two Springers who turned out to know a few facts about the central world of Baalol."

"Which world is it?" asked Atlan.

"We have the name of the sun it orbits. It's known as Aptut. It's supposed to be a binary star. The planet Trakarat is said to have rings around it like Saturn."

Atlan exchanged glances with Gen. Toseff. The Saratanian shook his head.

"I have never heard of such a system," said the Imperator.

Mercant spoke up. "It's supposed to be close to the center of the galaxy. I know that area isn't exactly lacking in other stars and planets but this system is unusual enough, perhaps, to have been listed with its coordinates in the catalogs. At any rate there must be some kind of information about it in the memory banks of the robot Regent.''

Bell hastily added: ''We wanted to ask you to help us in our search for Trakarat. The Regent's help would certainly make it easier to figure out the points of reference.''

Without hesitation Atlan gave him his assurance. ''I'll do all I can to locate this peculiar solar system.''

The Terrans' expressions of gratitude did him good. There he still saw his old true friends who would help him in any precarious situation. They suffered under the burden of Rhodan's illness as much as he.

''We'll transmit all the data we've picked up from the Springers,'' Bell told him. ''You'll get a full transcript of the entire hearing.''

''Every clue can be important,'' Atlan reminded him, ''no matter how small. You should cross-examine the Traders again.''

''Imperator,'' said Mercant solemnly, ''there's one thing I'll promise you. You know this action here was not of our own doing, so as soon as it's wrapped up the Solar Fleet will remove itself from sovereign territory of the Greater Imperium.''

They continued to discuss further details until Maj. Krefenbac advised that the 10 cruisers had come back and that Perry Rhodan was shuttling over to the *Ironduke* in a commuter craft. By special request of Reginald Bell the communication was cut off.

Atlan had become increasingly concerned over the description of Rhodan's illness and he decided to call his old friend personally after he had returned and taken over command of the *Ironduke* again. Even Bell's objections could not deter him from this decision.

After the connection with the Terran ship had been cut off,

Atlan turned to Gen. Toseff. "Once more we have avoided having a war between the two imperiums," he said.

"Wasn't the price a little too high, Your Eminence?" asked Toseff.

"Our prestige is still intact because the Solar Fleet will withdraw, so we can chalk it up to a military success that was achieved without bloodshed."

It was plain to see that the General might have wished to contradict him but either he was not sure of himself or his awe of Atlan was too great.

For some time they discussed the next steps that the undying Admiral would be taking and thus Gen. Toseff was gradually introduced to the whole plan and concept of rebuilding the Greater Imperium. The chief of the Saratan government came to see that Gonozal VIII intended to install Terran assistants everywhere. It could even be said theoretically that once a general agreement had been established the Greater Imperium would soon be strongly under Earthly influence, while the scope of power of the present decadent dignitaries would become limited.

Atlan concluded: "I'm convinced that once Rhodan has gotten his health back we'll quickly reestablish the old friendly relations. The Terran assistants will return to their previous positions and our mutual trust will be strengthened even more. Believe me, General, without the Terrans we won't be able to hold the Greater Imperium together. We need their help to keep us from falling apart into a countless number of little kingdoms and empires."

"I hope that your reasoning in this is correct, Your Highness," said Toseff.

"Now I wish to speak to my very sick friend," Atlan told him. "Try to contact the *Ironduke*, General."

When the viewscreen began to flicker after a few seconds Atlan could not suppress a certain tension in his solar plexus. Somehow it was a strange feeling to be seeing Rhodan again under these conditions. How would Perry react to his call?

The screen cleared up and he could see into the Control Central of the *Ironduke*. In the background he made out a number of officers who were seated at their control consoles. Then a figure came into view from one side and filled the screen. Atlan opened his mouth in horror and irrepressibly blurted out, "Oh no!" He had to force himself to continue looking at this apparition which had once been Perry Rhodan. The First Administrator of the Solar Imperium had turned into a shapeless giant with a bloated face.

"What do you want?" was the question he heard on his speaker.

The Imperator could only continue staring in consternation. "Perry!" he moaned. "I didn't know it was as bad as this!"

"You can keep all your pitying drivel, Arkonide," replied Cardif-Rhodan angrily. "If you have something to say then get on with it—but don't give me all that tearful old-woman blubbering!"

Atlan endured the abuse in silence. He didn't notice that Gen. Toseff's hands were gripping certain control levers in such rage that his knuckles turned white. At this moment Atlan was swearing to himself that he would help his deformed friend no matter what the cost.

"You may count on my complete support, Perry," he said, and he cut the connection before Rhodan could insult him further.

"You shouldn't have submitted to that, Imperator!" shouted Toseff, beside himself with outrage.

Atlan had a mental vision again of all the adventures that he and Rhodan had come thru together. He recalled their duel in the distant past and thought of the tacit understanding that had developed between them in the course of time. Of *these* things the General knew nothing. He only saw the present.

In the quiet interior of the robotship Atlan's voice sounded out with firm determination. "He is my friend, General, and I will do all I can to save him."

Toseff knew then that nothing would stand in the way of the Imperator's decision. Quietly he left the Control Central. He knew when a man wanted to be by himself. He appreciated the magnitude of Atlan's responsibility.

300 ADVENTURES FROM NOW
Clark Darlton will introduce you to
Friends from an Alien Universe

THE SHIP OF THINGS TO COME

GRIMLY, Bell spoke.

"I won't hold anything back, Atlan. We're at the brink of disaster.

"Trouble is starting to brew in the Fleet officers' corps. Even some of the mutants, our most important people—

"A revolt is taking shape!

"If there's to be any hope of saving the Solar Imperium, we have to place Rhodan in protective custody immediately."

Rhodan in protective custody? But there must be a million troops blindly committed to the Administrator!

The explosive situation leads next issue to—

DUEL UNDER THE DOUBLE SUN

By

K.-H. Scheer

An Atlan Adventure

400 ADVENTURES FROM NOW
See *Solitude's Guardians*

THE TIME VAULT

An Ackerman Recovery
EXPERIMENT IN GENIUS
Part 3

(Conclusion)
By William F. Temple
(Author of "HGWells Slept Here" &
"Forrest Jolson Sings Again")*

*THE INTRIGUED READER is advised not to search second-hand bookstores for these titles (nor the author's autobiography, *I Am Zorro!*) as the titles are non-existent & an inside joke.

No joke is the conclusion to this powerful psychological story of the year 2443 as seen thru the extrapolative optics of William F. Temple, a science fiction byline which belongs in the pantheon of Wells, Clarke, Wyndham, Stapledon & Orwell.

* * * *

4

The placid surface of the civilization of 2443 A.D. was becoming ruffled. For, although the first three men who had been told of the impending doom had kept silent about it, their informant hadn't. Bruce Lion gave an interview to the press and told the world that its days were numbered; he added that it would not be long before he published the exact number.

Ripples of agitation spread when the Millan-Thorne equation story broke and Professor Hurst refused to confirm or deny it. The people reasoned, correctly, that he would have denied it had he been able to. And then the people began to realize that what passed for scientists in their world were no source of help at all. These pundits could tell you about anything that *had* happened in Science, but they seemed unable to extrapolate any of this into the future. Nobody had thought much about the future, for to do so in a practically changeless world was pointless. The habit of living in the present was strong upon all, laymen and scientists alike. The future to them was an endless Today.

And now, suddenly, the future had reared up over them like a black threat. Tomorrow might not, after all, be another Today. Today's sunset might be the last they would ever see.

And even the State Nurses couldn't help them.

Their ancestors, inured to hardship, disappointment, and catastrophe after catastrophe, would have made a better showing. But this generation, product of the soft green lawns, watched over and shielded since infancy, feeling settled and secure in the best of all possible worlds, lacked the fibre to accept sentence of horrible death with equanimity.

Nervous disorders sprang up everywhere in a world which had been free from them for centuries. The people just could not face the fact that at any moment they might become ashes among the ashes of their paradise. And so they dodged it; they took refuse in amnesia, or hedonism, or drugs, or strange creeds and pseudo-philosophies.

The mostly widely supported of the pseudo-philosophies became known as the "Ignorance is Bliss" movement. Its leader said:

"Knowledge has caused more misery to mankind than anything else. The more you are aware of, the more you have to

worry about. Man was happy in the Garden of Eden before he picked the forbidden fruit from the Tree of Knowledge. Do not let us repeat that mistake; let us refuse to know the name of the day on which this world is doomed. Bruce Lion must never reveal the date. For if he does he will destroy hope, and we shall be as people already dead. While there is hope, there is life. For all we know at present, this disaster may not happen for centuries yet. Let us ask Bruce Lion to keep his silence for the sake of us all."

So a deputation was formed, headed by the leader, and they approached Bruce.

"Sir, we beg of you, in the name of humanity, to abandon your calculations. Leave us at least the solace of hope."

Bruce regarded the little knot of men inscrutably. Then he said: "I have some advice for you."

"Yes?" said the leader, eagerly.

"I advise you all to leave for the Sahara Desert immediately."

There was a murmur of excitement.

"Is that a safe area?" asked the leader, even more eagerly.

"Yes, for you and your kind; you'll have to take special precautions, of course."

"Of course. Of what nature?"

"You all kneel on the sand, and with your hands you scoop out little holes just in front of you. Then you all bury your heads in the sand."

The leader stared at him, disappointed and puzzled. The eyes behind Bruce's thick lenses showed no trace of humor.

"Oh," said the leader, doubtfully. "Is there nothing else?"

"Only one thing more. Tomorrow I reckon to finish my calculations. I shall know the exact date then. *And so shall you!* Good afternoon, gentlemen."

They protested in dismay, and Bruce walked away and left them.

The psychologist and the Biologist heard about it.

"I thought he lacked a sense of humor," said the Psychologist, "but he seems to have one of a sort—bitter and sardonic. I'm afraid he's not really human. How he must relish getting his own back on all of us like this! Well, I suppose we asked for it."

"You and I did—but not the others."

"I hold no brief for the others," said the Psychologist; "I must say I'm ashamed to belong to such a race of cowards."

"Say rather frightened children. It's not their fault. This is not a civilization which breeds men. The point is, what are responsible people like ourselves going to do about it?"

"What *can* we do?"

"If you had a child with *angina pectoris,* and you knew to within a day when he was likely to drop dead, would you tell him which day would be his last?"

"Of course not," said the Psychologist. "I'd let him play in his innocence as long as possible. I see your parallel—it's a good one. They *are* children, and we must do our best to see they're treated as children. We must argue it out with Bruce—"

"Do you really believe we'll move him?"

The Psychologist considered. "No," he admitted, "I don't. We're the last people to try it; he hates us down to the backbone."

"Exactly. There's one person who might touch his heart: Freda."

"Freda? I wonder . . . Has she married?"

"No."

"I'll get on to New Washington, and have her come by air right away," said the Psychologist.

She approached him as he sat writing at his usual desk in the corner of the Library. "Bruce!" she said, and stopped as she saw that the little man was trembling. He kept his gaze down on his work, but his pen moved aimlessly over the page, producing nothing but meaningless squiggles.

"Bruce, are you ill?" she said, concernedly, and came beside him.

"No," he said, gruffly. He took off his glasses and wiped them. Only then did he look up. His face was expressionless.

"What do you want?"

"I want to make a personal appeal for you to keep your discoveries to yourself. Please."

"Oh. Another ostrich."

"I'm not thinking of myself. I'm thinking of the people at large. Do this at least for them."

"Why should I care about them? What did they care about me?"

"*They* had nothing to do with it. It was a committee of the Administration. You can't blame everybody; you can't hate the whole world because of an imagined injustice committed by a few."

"Can't I?" he said, grimly.

"If you do, it shows evidence of a warped mentality—a psycho-neurotic."

"That's exactly what the Psychologist and the Biologist were trying to make of me, wasn't it? Is it my fault if they succeeded?"

"You've been told a hundred times that their intentions were for the good of us all. Must you nurse a grudge forever? You above all people must know that there's only one thing in this world that matters—something more important than cold intellect, or impassioned art, or childish grievances. And that's kindness."

"Tell that to your two friends. They sent you, didn't they?"

"They asked me to come."

"And once they asked you to go. And you went. Do you always do as they ask—and never as I ask?"

"What did you ever ask me, Bruce?"

"I didn't put it into words; I was young and incoherent then. I've aged a lot these last few years. But I made my feelings for you plain. And you ignored me, and left me—to them."

And suddenly Freda saw through all his defenses, his grimness and sarcasm, his apparent preoccupation with work, to the lonely and abandoned boy who hid behind them. She put her arm about him comfortingly. He didn't resist, but he wouldn't look at her. His pen traced some more meaningless designs.

"I'm sorry, Bruce. I was wrong; I shouldn't have let them come between us with their specious arguments. I thought they were right, but they were not. If you wrong an individual, you have done wrong, and all the talking in the world can't change its nature. The State exists for the individual—it's not the other way round. All good, all progress flowers from the individual, not from masses. They realized that, and they tried to create an individual who might flower for the general benefit. But they robbed you of your real individuality, made a warped, unhappy creature out of you. I don't care in whose name they did it—they were wrong."

He ignored all that. "Why didn't you ever come and see me? Or even write? I never had another word from you."

"I thought it was wrong to do so, and I hoped you'd forget me."

"Forget you! Not a day has passed since when I haven't ached to see you again."

"Never mind," she said. "We shall see each other every day now—until the last day."

He mused for a time. "F-Freda," he said suddenly, his old

stutter momentarily returning. "W-Will you marry me? They w-wouldn't stop it now on health grounds—their own f-future isn't so healthy."

"Yes, Bruce. On one condition—that you tear up all these old figures and forget them. If we're to have a little happiness ourselves now, we can't make thousands of others unhappy."

Bruce picked up the sheets he'd been working on, ripped them across several times, and dropped them in the waste basket.

"I'll do more than that," he said. "I'll do my best to make them happy. I'll see if I can think of a way out for us all."

"Oh, Bruce! . . . "

5

And so Bruce Lion married. The world got to know that he was working now on the salvation of all, and it calmed down considerably. Bruce Lion was a peculiar man, but he was a genius—the only one in the world. On his brain depended all their lives. They began to regard him as a superman, almost as a god. They referred to him, without irony, as "Our Genius," and his every movement was news.

Presently the news-seekers had a real story: Freda Lion was going to have a baby.

Happiness returned to the world.

"If doomsday were to be soon, he would never have had a child," people smiled. "He must be optimistic about things—I expect he's found the way to save us."

But the next story to break dispelled all the happiness.

By a million to one chance, something went wrong with the birth. Freda died—and her son lived. And Bruce Lion became something scarcely distinguishable from a madman.

He locked himself away with the child, and for months the

world saw little of him. When it did see him, no intelligent word could be got from him. Those who attempted to speak to him were either ignored or made the victims of incoherent abuse. He went about the State Buildings with a face almost unrecognizable as his own: sometimes it was gray with pain or grief, sometimes it was set in lines of cold ferocity or flushed with wild rage. And sometimes it was the face of an imbecile, stupid, empty.

Later, he came out more frequently, and then at length resumed his daily work in the Library or the Laboratories. But he remained unapproachable. He snarled at those who came near him, and sometimes when his experiments seemed to go wrong he would have fits of destructive frenzy. The Laboratory assistants began to dread his taking apparatus—he no longer asked for it, but took it. And each evening he returned alone to his apartment and his son.

Said the Biologist one day: "It's time something was done about Bruce. We know a person of his super-sensitive nature must feel grief more keenly than any of us. We know he idolized Freda, and she was his whole life. But . . . it can't go on like this. I'm beginning to fear that grief has unhinged his mind permanently. It's your job, you know. You should take him in hand."

"My dear fellow," said the Psychologist, "I might as well try to take a hurricane in hand. He curses me green every time I try to go near him. Only yesterday I stopped him and suggested that we have a little chat, and that I thought I could help him. He just sneered: 'I've had all I want of *your* help, thank you.' And when I protested, he rounded on me and said: 'Look, do you want me to save your precious hide along with those of the other creatures that crawl over this planet?' I said I supposed so. And he snarled: 'Then for heaven's sake get yourself and your mumbo-jumbo out of my way, and let me get on with my work!' You know, I think the child should go to a State Nursery.''

"It's very difficult," said the Biologist, scratching his head. "Children can't be brought up in the Nurseries without the parents' consent. Of course, we know that ninety per cent of the parents give it—they're only too glad to be freed of the responsibility of the children. But we can't take children away from parents who can't bear to be parted from them. It's obvious that Bruce has transferred his overwhelming love for Freda to her child, he clings to him because it's all that's left of her. Well, I suppose it's all right. It's possible to smother a child with too much love, but at the same time it's very difficult to do so: children will absorb all the love you give them. The boy is visited by a State Nurse every day, and she reports that he's in excellent health. I'm afraid we can only leave things to take their course.''

Things took their course in much the same way for several years. The only change was that gradually Bruce lost regard as the hope of the world. He seemed still to be working hard, but he made no reports on the progress of his work, and people began to fall again to doubt and despair. *Was* Bruce Lion still working on their salvation, or had he abandoned them? Or—as looked most likely from his behavior—had he gone out of his mind?

Then one day they all went mad with joy, because he announced that he thought he was nearing the solution of the problem of mankind's safety, and hoped to let them know in a week's time.

"It's seems as if we're going to be justified, after all," said the Psychologist.

"Well, it's a comforting thing to believe, so let's believe it,'' said the Biologist.

At the end of the week Bruce asked for a meeting of the Administration. It was granted only too willingly. When this body of scholarly advisors and social managers had assembled in the Council Chamber, Bruce mounted the dais, still a diminutive figure, more stooped than ever, and with hair already graying.

"Gentlemen, I've called this meeting because I believe this is an historic moment. The sun's transformation into a nova is due at no distant date, and there's nothing I can do about stopping that. As you can imagine, it's beyond human power, genius or no genius. However, there's no need for us all to say here to be cremated. We have the rocket-ships and we have the time to shift, in relays, the whole of Earth's population—thankfully, it's but an infinitesimal percentage of what it was before the Wars so drastically diminished it.

"I've heard it suggested that as the solar system provides no sanctuary, we should try to reach the nearer stars. Now, the nearest star is four and a quarter light-years away, and it has no planetary system. As far as we know, the nearest planetary system is nearly twenty light-years away. The best speed at which our rocket-ships can travel is ten miles per second. At top speed, therefore, it would take, at the very least, 300,000 years to reach that system. 300,000 years in a crowded rocketship with limited air! It's preposterous, of course. We've got to seek a lot nearer home. There's only one answer: Pluto.

"I know what you're thinking—Pluto's atmosphere is thick with a deadly virus. So is the atmosphere of this planet of ours: there are a great many kinds of bacterial floating in it fatal to anyone not immunised against them, as we are by long experience and adaptation. For years I've been experimenting with the cultures we have of the Plutonic virus, and now at last I think I have the answer."

He held up a hypodermic syringe, and there was a great buzz of excitement. "Just a solution of certain chemicals. Easy enough when you know the answer—but endless trial and error was the only path to that answer. The virus gets into the bloodstream through the lungs, and there it flourishes—unless it's unfortunate enough to encounter these chemicals, which kill it instantly. I propose that when we land on Pluto, we shall all have prepared just this reception for the Plutonic virus. One injection of this preparation should provide immunity for a year, before the body completely absorbs it. And then, of course, it can always be replaced. I propose now to give myself the first annual injection."

He bared his arm, inserted the needle, and pressed the plunger. There was absolute silence as he rolled his sleeve down. "I did not remark on it," he said, "but there is a slight risk attached to this. It had not been tried on a human being before one minute ago. If I had mentioned it, it's probable that the Administration would have insisted that my life was too valuable to risk, and that some poor non-genius must be used for a guinea pig. Now, I happen to feel very strongly about that sort of thing. I myself was once the victim of an experiment, and because of it I seek no victims for my own experiments. The right of a civilization to knowledge does *not* include the right to risk or ruin an individual's life—unless the individual understands and agrees. Pasteur injected himself with his own serums. The discoverer of chloroform tried it on himself first. Unfortunately, there are so-called scientists who prize their own skins far too highly to risk them, and prefer to satisfy their curiosity with some innocent and helpless victim."

There was iron in this last jibe, and up in the public gallery the Psychologist and the Biologist wriggled and avoided each other's eyes.

"However, I don't want to sound dramatic," resumed Bruce. "I'm pretty sure that the preparation is quite harmless so far as human beings are concerned, else I should not have called this meeting. Now, about Pluto. I think Pluto can be made inhabitable. It's a cold and dark planet, we know, and will be colder and darker yet when the sun has died down to a smaller star after its blaze. But we have the secrets of atomic energy. We can crowd into a limited area of the planet and heat it and light it sufficiently for ourselves. It won't be as naturally beautiful as Earth, but we can create our own beauty. It's up to us to rebuild our sort of world. It won't be easy, but we can do it. If we have the faith, we are people with a future."

There was a spontaneous outburst of applause at this. It lasted for several minutes, and Bruce stood there silently, his brown eyes alight behind his spectacles. And then a faint smile touched his lips.

"Good Lord, d'you see that?" whispered the Psychologist to the Biologist, while they both clapped hard. "He smiled! I've never seen him smile before—never!"

Bruce held up his hand and applause died down. "All that remains to be done—" he said, and then suddenly he put both hands to his chest and flung back his head with a loud, indrawn gasp which made everyone jump. His face became twisted with agony. He teetered on the edge of the dais.

People scrambled up to get to him.

"Freda! Fre—" he jerked out, and then pitched forward off the dais. He hit the floor, sprawling face-downwards, breaking his nose. But it did not matter. The only pair of spectacles in the world smashed into splinters. It did not matter—their need was finished.

The Chairman got to him first, and knelt beside him for a long minute.

When he arose, he climbed slowly onto the dais, and made a solemn announcement: "While we live," he said, "we have to honor the name of Bruce Lion. For he was not merely a martyr to Science—he died for us all."

No one could discover just what killed Bruce Lion. Doctors examined the hypodermic he used, and found it empty. There was not a trace left of the chemicals it had contained—he must have injected every drop of the solution. Yet, when they performed an autopsy on his body, they found nothing foreign in the blood which responded to any tests they knew. What was this mysterious stuff which defied detection and analysis?

They hoped to get a clue from the five hundred and twenty-three notebooks which Bruce had left. Each book was crammed to the covers with close writing, but it was writing in a cipher which defeated all the experts, although they spent years in trying to break it down. In any case, they were looking for something which at the most could be only of partial help, for Bruce had made an error somewhere, either in the composition or the size of the dose. And who could succeed where he had failed?

The dark age of despair came clouding down again.

The scrambles for pleasure began again, but after ten years of gathering the rosebuds while they may (with one apprehensive eye cocked the while at the sun overhead, and a panic at every sun-spot) the people fell into a mood of dull resignation. They had exhausted their capacity for worrying, but they could regain the spontaneous happiness and peace of mind which had been theirs in the golden days when no sword of Damocles hung over their heads.

To them nothing seemed worth doing any more. What was the use of beginning anything, even the smallest task, if there was always this sizeable chance that one might never live to finish it, nor anyone left to take over from where one left off? It was a sullen, apathetic world.

The Psychologist was sitting alone in his apartment one day glowering through the window at the sunlight striking flaming color from the flowerbeds ringing the lawn. (Neither the flowerbeds nor the lawn were anything like so tidy as once they had been—only a born fool would spend his last days weeding.)

He was mentally composing a poem of blank verse, which he would never finish or write down because—well, what was the use? The opening of it ran:

"O, treacherous Sun, with thy false promise,
Luring while waiting to strike . . ."

And then suddenly the Biologist flung himself into the room. There was no other word for it. The door shot open and the Biologist came in like a whirling dervish. He tripped and spun and fell on his knees, and the sheets of typescript he was carrying flew up and then came floating down all over the room like great flakes of snow. He crawled around collecting them feverishly, his face alive with excitement.

"What on earth! . . . " said the Psychologist.

A shapeless wad of manuscript was thrust into his lap, "Read this," said the Biologist, urgently. "I've just had it from the author, before it goes to press. That's the first batch—I'll get 'em in order . . . "

The psychologist read. It was an untitled manuscript, a short book of not more than 30,000 words. But it was concise, tight-packed with information, data, and documented proofs.

It set out to make a point, and it hammered that point home with an impressive weight of facts and checked statements, verified calculations, proof by argument, proof by psychological instances and parallels. And the point was that Bruce Lion had never been a mathematical or scientific genius at all, but merely a great bluff.

It showed beyond doubt that Bruce had *not* solved the Millan-Thorne equation, but only made a cunning show of having done so: his sheets of calculations were a deliberate plant; he knew he was being watched. He'd just copied the first half of the equation from Taft's *Electron Paths*, supplanting the usual symbols by meaningless ones. The second half and the resolution were just a fake, a hodge-podge of pretended calculations which looked impressive but meant precisely nothing. Similarly, all the writings in the notebooks were gibberish: there was no cipher.

The credit for the completion of the equation should actually go to Professor Hurst. Trying to form sense out of Bruce's nonsense, the solution had suddenly occurred to him. He thought he'd been inspired to it by Bruce's symbols, but that was only a coincidence. The professor had spent a great deal of time in the past grappling with that same famous problem: his subconscious mind had been at work on it continually, and solved it, and divulged the solution while he was poring over Bruce's so-called calculations.

Bruce Lion was a born opportunist, said the author. *He seized on the prestige arising from that lucky chance to make the world cower before him. He donned a Hallowe'en mask, and in a solemn and awful voice warned the world of its impending doom. And because scientists everywhere took him at Professor Hurst's valuation, and thought that he understood things beyond their comprehension, they accepted his flapdoodle as gospel truth.*

(Here the author presented convincing astro-physical grounds for the sun's not becoming a nova for at least another hundred million years.)

He went on: *Why did Bruce Lion pretend to be a master scientist when he was not? The reason was that he was trying to compensate for the terrific inferiority feelings which had been inculcated in him, and he felt that he must be better at something than anyone else in the world, a champion, This, of course, is exactly what the experimenters intended. But there was one drawback; Bruce Lion had no natural creative talent whatever, nor any particular ability for inductive or deductive reasoning. He could absorb knowledge easily, but he lacked the ability to use it to discover new knowledge. He felt strongly, but was by nature insufficiently integrated to be able to express his feelings in any form worthy of the name of art—except, perhaps, one, which will be mentioned. Yet he was driven by this overpowering urge to gain respect.*

In particular he did want the respect of one person, Freda Mann, a Laboratory assistant, for he had fallen in love with her. She was a conscientious worker, with a great respect for the Laboratory chiefs. Bruce Lion made up his mind that somehow he would become her boss, so that she would similarly look up to him. Which meant that he had to become a notable scientist—or appear to be one. To his poor uncoordinated mind, the appearance was as good as the reality—if enough people could be persuaded to believe in the appearance. Well, he succeeded in persuading enough of us.

But he did not succeed with Freda, because she was removed from his reach. This was the bitterest blow dealt him so far. He fell into a fury of hatred against the society which treated him as a pariah, which had filled him with frustration and bitter despair. He resolved to pay society back in its own coin, and he succeeded in full measure. One can hardly avoid the conclusion that society had reaped what it had sown.

He gained Freda later, only to lose her again. So as not to lose her cherished respect, he had invented more mythical scientific research work, and the pose was now to be the saviour of the world. It is difficult now to tell how far fact and fantasy were confused in his mind at that time, but it is certain that later he went through whole periods when he could not distinguish them apart. Freda's death almost completely unhinged him. For years afterwards he lived in the twilight world on the frontiers of insanity. And at last he decided that without Freda life for him was no longer worth the living.

Because he was what he was, he planned to make his suicide a spectacular one, holding his audience to the last. His warped, approval-starved mind demanded an exit to applause. He got it, as we know—and he even smiled in that brief triumph.

He displayed a fair amount of ingenuity with his story of the immunisation to the Plutonic virus. Actually, the hypodermic syringe he used on himself was empty of anything except air. He deliberately injected a large bubble of air into his bloodstream, which, when it reached his heart, stopped it. He fell dead, an indetectable suicide.

Summing up, there is one talent which we must concede to Bruce Lion: he was an actor of no mean ability. Indeed, there is little doubt that this was his natural line had he followed it instead of deviating into science because of his love for Freda: it led to his desperately plying his only talent in entirely the wrong environment. One might claim that it was more than talent, that only an actor of genius could fool the whole world for so long. And his greatest role was his last one—The Martyr.

The Psychologist finished the book, and sat for some time staring into space.

"Well," said the Biologist, "What do you think of it?"

The Psychologist roused himself. "It's terrific," he said, quietly. "Absolutely authentic, too—you can see that. This book is going to set the world free from its bondage to despair and dispel its sense of futility. We can all begin to live again. It's a masterpiece of research and documentation, analysis and deduction. The author is undoubtedly a genius. Who is he?''

''A fellow who had an unusual upbringing in childhood and an unusual parent. A parent whose fame towered over the boy like a Colossus, and made him feel very small indeed. A parent of unpredictable moods and frenzies, who was often quite mad and always overbearing and crushing. A parent who hated his son fiercely, and piled guilt upon his shoulders, constantly, unceasingly, because the boy's birth had killed the beloved Freda.''

''So Bruce Lion hated his son,'' said the Psychologist, slowly, ''and all the time we thought he cherished him.''

''Luckily, he was of a tougher fibre than his father. He suffered, but he kept his balance—and he observed and recorded, for the sake of all of us.''

''Well, we produced a real genius, after all,'' said the Psychologist, ''even if we did have to take the long way around . . .''

The Biologist rubbed his eyes. ''I wouldn't be too sure. I wonder if we haven't been going at it from the wrong angle. We found frustration as a common denominator in the geniuses of the past, so we decided that it was a necessary factor. . . . But, what did we do to frustrate Bruce? *We just systematically applied every type of personality shock that was common to people in the old days*. They all got that sort of thing, to one degree or another—a few got as full a dose as Bruce did, although perhaps not with the same intent or precision.''

The other man shook his head. ''But then, how do you account for the fact that, without this nasty conditioning, Utopia produced no geniuses?''

"It has been occurring to me that sheer, overpowering benevolence can be damnably frustrating. We applied the knock-down method; perhaps Utopia is just smothering the kids. It doesn't warp them—it just anesthetizes them. . . . You know, Bruce *was* a genius, in his own way—and all the great ones have been, in their own way. But we blocked off every healthy way he could express himself."

"But," objected the Psychologist, "what about Lion's son? He wasn't smothered with kindness, and he seems to have had a rough time of it, too."

"Rough—yes—but not quite as hellish as the rigorous, scientifically worked-out course we gave Lion. They're both geniuses—in *spite* of the frustrations . . . Do you think he'll dedicate his book to us?"

THE END

500 ADVENTURES FROM NOW
William Voltz describes
Danger: Andromeda

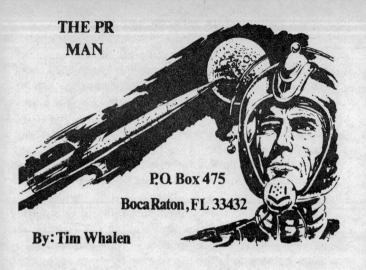

THE PR MAN

P.O. Box 475
Boca Raton, FL 33432

By: Tim Whalen

OPERATION: CONPAK

Here are a few news releases from Rhofandom and also general science fiction fandom. Hopefully they will give you a better idea of what is going on in fandom.

First of all, ARKON-Los Angeles is in temporary stasis. Convention Chairman H.J.N. Andruschak is looking for a hotel and a good date to hold the convention. We are hoping to be able to have Walter Ernsting, Forry & Wendayne Ackerman and Sig Wahrman as our guests. If you are anxious to receive the most up-to-date information, you can get it in *Rhocomzine*, (available from Editor, Henry Davis, Jr., Baker Station Rd., Goodlettesville/TN 37072. Sample copy is 75¢). Hopefully ARKON-Los Angeles will be a nice small PERRY RHODAN convention where the attendees will be able to mingle with the guests, as at RHOCON 1. Keep tuned in for more information on the West Coast's first PERRY RHODAN convention.

Some of you out there might be interested in holding small, one-day PERRY RHODAN conventions in your hometowns. These are not meant to be with guests (if so, you would be talking about spending over $5000) but some of you might like to sponsor a small convention/meeting for 50 or 100 Rhofans. This type of "conlet" might cost $300 to $500. You would show a few films, have a few discussions about PERRY RHO-DAN, and similar things. If you are *seriously* interested in putting on a small convention of this type. Rhocom is putting together an information packet which tells you where to obtain films, how to go about getting a hotel and how to manage advertising, etc. This information packet will cost $3.50. If you do decide to go ahead with the convention, be assured that you will receive an announcement in these pages, with place, date, some information about your convention and a contact where people may write for information on your con. This conpak is currently available. Send your order to the address for THE PR MAN.

600 ADVENTURES FROM NOW
H.G. Ewers describes the
War of the SOL

Shock Short

ALIEN TRAP? Tunnelvision becomes terrorvision in this "First" by a rabid Rhofan that will *make your flesh crawl* . . .

TUNNEL
by Roger Aday

"What kind of tunnel is it?" asked Greg, following Terry and Alan down the steep hill.

"We don't know. It's big, tho," said Terry. "You can walk upright in it!"

"I wonder where it leads."

"We'll find out," said Alan. "Terry and I found it yesterday but didn't want to explore it until you could come too."

The 3 young men made their way to the bottom of the hill and Alan went straight to where the entrance lay. "It's dark," he called. "Get out your flashlights!"

Greg pulled his out and flipped it on. As he peered into the tunnel, his thin beam of light showed all there was to see.

The dark passageway, which was obviously man-made and walled with cement, led back about 10 feet, then turned off to the left and right.

"Let's go," said Alan and stepped into the tunnel.

Terry and Greg followed and were soon at the bend. They

peered around the corner and shined their flashlights to see if there were more turnoffs. None could be seen.

"I'm writing my initials on the wall here so we'll know which entrance leads back out!" said Alan and wrote AB on the wall.

"Which direction should we go?" wondered Terry, looking both ways.

"Let's go right," suggested Greg and took over the lead. On and on they went. As far as they could see was nothing but more tunnel.

"What was this made for?" ventured Alan after they'd walked quite awhile.

"I don't know but it's getting smaller," said Greg. "I could stand upright in it when we started. Now I'm having to bend over."

"He's right," said Terry. "Let's go the other way. My back is starting to hurt from walking hunched over."

All were in agreement so they started back. They hadn't gone far when Terry spoke up once more.

"Something's wrong," he said. "The tunnel should start getting bigger but I'll swear it's still getting smaller."

"It has to be your imagination," retorted Greg but he'd noticed it also. They kept on and were soon forced to crawl on their hands and knees.

They were on the verge of having to scoot along on their stomachs when Alan called out. "I've found an opening!"

They all crowded around with much difficulty to the hole Alan had discovered.

"What good is that?" asked Greg. "We can't even begin to fit into that thing."

"We have to be going in the wrong direction," said Terry. It's only logical that if we go back the other direction, the tunnel will get bigger."

Greg was on the verge of agreeing when Alan called out.

"Oh, my god!"

"What is it?"

But Alan could say no more. He merely pointed.

Greg bent down and saw what he was pointing at. Next the tiny opening, almost too small to read, were the initials AB in white chalk!

TIME VAULT TWO

CLYDE CRANE CAMPBELL was a name to conjure with in the Golden Age of Scientifiction.

Small wonder—we were eventually to learn he was (and is!) Horace L. Gold!

In introducing this story, which we revive in 2 parts, the great *Astounding* editor F. Orlin Tremaine said:

"Mighty in its scope, this Thought-variant tells of the most bewildering cataclysm ever to overtake the home of man."

An Ackerman Archival Recovery par excellence is—

INFLEXURE

LANSE threw his head back with a sudden snap and stood dazed for an instant. His hand, hovering above a mass of scrawled paper, shook. The vacant look of incomprehension faded from his watery eyes; they filled with fear. He let his breath out with a low trembling whistle.

Still shaking, he turned swiftly around to face Worthing, who sat amazed at the odd actions of his usually phlegmatic friend.

"Do you believe in God?" Lanse demanded brusquely.

Worthing gasped. "Why? What?"

Lanse muttered savagely: "Retribution—they'll call it retribution. And maybe they won't be far wrong." He shrugged and collapsed into a chair. He laughed shortly, ironically.

"Something happen?" Worthing asked.

"Not yet!"

Worthing relaxed visibly.

"I thought perhaps I was going crazy," Lanse went on. "Checked and rechecked. Same result every time. Not that there's so much to check up on," he pointed out to Worthing, shaking his finger emphatically. A note of despair edged into his voice. "It'd be better if there was, I think. Then I'd have a margin of doubt. But like this I——"

Worthing kept silent, letting his friend talk. In his opinion, Lanse was headed for a breakdown, tortured as he was by financial insecurity and lack of recognition as well as self-imposed overwork. The astronomical physicist was young—not more than thirty—yet already his thin hair was graying, the lines on his drawn face etching deeper almost visibly.

If Lanse would only come up to his—Worthing's—summer home in the mountains for a month or so, he'd come back twenty pounds to the good and feeling a thousand times keener. Hardly! Lanse was too independent; wanted to make his own way, he said.

"Look at this photograph," Lanse ordered, shoving a large square of brilliantly glazed paper toward Worthing.

A large circle of unvarying white brightness extended nearly to the edges of the photograph; around the globe a black background lightened evenly until it approached what was evidently a reflected whiteness. Worthing thought he recognized in it the Sun, but, on closer scrutiny, the huge spots of swirling darkness seemed to suggest Jupiter.

"That's old Sol," Lanse announced tersely. "And here's another smiling snap, taken during the winter."

Three lines had been drawn on the picture; one through the center, two at each outside extremity. It took Worthing a little time to realize the importance of these lines. Something appeared wrong with the photograph when he first looked at it. Of course! He glanced very closely at it. The line at the left had been drawn on a tangent parallel with the center line, but the right one cut through the circle a quarter of an inch from the perimeter.

Then he noticed two double-headed arrows, marking a radius from each side. The distance quoted on the two arrows from outside tangents to diameter were exactly equal, as his eye agreed. Then if that was so—the Sun was lopsided.

"Exactly!" Lanse nodded, when he saw the astounded look in his friend's eyes. "Something is pulling the Sun out of shape. A gigantic force is being exerted on it."

"Do you know what it is?" Worthing whispered.

"I have an excellent idea. Listen, if this sounds idiotic and fantastic, don't blame me. There's no other explanation.

"A force that could distort the Sun that much must be either tremendously large or else dangerously close, or both. But where is it? I have photographs—Mount Wilson photographs, taken within the last three weeks—of the entire heavens, even the parts that couldn't possibly account for the force that's distorting the Sun. I couldn't take any chances of ignoring anything. But there's nothing——

"These pictures are reversed, you know. I'm just telling you that so you can realize this is a photograph of the Sun's profile. This one—the distortion. Here's the way that fact comes in: If you face Vega, which is approximately the center of our universe, every astronomical object in the universe is rotating from right to left, or east to west, and traveling around Vega in the same direction.

"Therefore, ordinarily a force that could pull the Sun out of shape like that would tear the planets away first, since it must approach from the right and the planets at that season when this picture were taken were mostly in that direction. So, as any well-behaved object would do, this colossal force should travel from the right as it approached the Sun, thus tearing every one of the planets out of its orbit, before it could reach the Sun.

"But it doesn't. This force is traveling in the opposite direction.

"Do you know what that means? I don't either, but I can guess. Take into consideration the fact that not a single star is blotted out in any field around or behind the Sun. Also, the sun-spot period was over five years ago and isn't due for another six years. According to precedent, there should be a very few tiny sun spots at this time. But take a look at the picture. The spots are vast, and every day they're widening and absorbing each other, so that they almost look like the red spot of Jupiter.

"And come over here and listen to this——"

Worthing followed him into the living room, standing to one side nervously as Lanse tuned in the radio. He whirled the knob aimlessly, shifting from one station to another. In points between the stations a steady hum sounded from the powerful radio, rising to a sudden shriek and scream of a million tortured demons that drowned out the most persistent programs as he set the dial on a broadcasting station.

"You've never heard static like that before," Lanse pointed out, straightening up and shutting off the power. "And that isn't the only thing.

"At around five in the afternoon—any afternoon—people as far south as Maryland can see the aurora twisting brightly in the sky, regardless of the Sun. Even during the highest peak of sun spots, when there's a violent electric storm around the north pole, it's an unusual occurrence to see the aurora any farther south than upper New York State.''

Worthing interrupted anxiously: ''I know all that. The papers are full of it every day.''

''Certainly! They can't afford to ignore such important phenomena. But do they carry the thing on to its natural conclusion? Of course not! They can't.

''Now the distortion of the Sun,'' he went on rapidly, ''is the first clue. Remember that's as though a titanic tide was being raised on the wrong side of the Sun, in the opposite direction from which the force should be exerted. Then remember that the body that's pulling the face of the Sun out of shape is completely invisible—not a dark star, for even a dark star would be visible at that distance, because of the star fields that would be blotted out. In this case, though, despite the fact that if we wait a few hours we can see the fields just hidden by the Sun, not a single star is invisible.

''All that is amazing enough. But more than that—this body is traveling in exactly the opposite direction from that of every other astronomical body in the universe.

''So I put all this together and shoved it aside for a while, until I could plot the erratic orbits of Mercury and Venus and the height of the tide raised on the Sun. In this way I discovered that the object is approximately the size of the Sun, at an unknown distance—less than a billion miles away, anyhow—and traveling at an unknown speed.''

''You couldn't find the speed?'' Worthing echoed.

''We're not Merlins,'' Lanse snapped testily. ''The star is invisible, so I couldn't gauge the variations in the spectrum's red line. And the orbital errors and the solar tide remain constant. How else can I find the speed? Let me finish——

''I added two and two and got an astronomical twenty two. But then,'' he brushed his hand across his tired eyes, ''there's so much that's contrary to what we've been accustomed to call fact.

"The best I could figure was that this invisible star that's traveling in the wrong direction is—a fourth-dimensional star." He finished slowly and stared at Worthing to see how he would take it.

Worthing permitted himself a half smile of disbelief. "You're joking, of course."

Lanse raised his aching, tired shoulders and dropped them hopelessly. "Have it your way," he mumbled.

"But, man, you're not serious!" Worthing cried.

"Isn't this a funny joke?" Lanse demanded angrily. "Do you think I'm going to spend six months or more, go to the expense of having dozens of Mount Wilson exposures made for me, and work like a dog on bewildering mathematics, just for the sake of seeing you smile? Don't be a fool! I was never more serious in my life."

Worthing sat silent for a while, stunned. The tiny workroom seemed oppressive. He wanted to get out into the open air—to stare up at the Sun and assure himself that the universe was all right.

"What will happen?" he asked softly.

Lanse gazed bitterly out of the window. A haze of dirty yellow light struggled between the narrow space of the two tenement houses. His glance rested on dusty red brick.

"Who knows?" He turned to Worthing, his tired watery eyes behind their thick glasses were enormous. "There's a good chance for our being totally destroyed, and not much for our survival. What happens when two stars collide?" He spread his hands. "Perhaps a few atoms are left to mark off the space, or a sun several times as large as the two individual stars. In either case—death!"

Neither moved for a while, thinking of the immediate future.

Suddenly Lanse raised his head and laughed—a weird cackle of sheer despair.

"Nothing matters any more," he said hollowly. "Money —fame—— Let's take that trip up to your summer home that you've been annoying me about for so long. We'll be well browned and in swell condition when old man death cuts the ground from under us."

II.

LANSE felt the warm rays of the Sun on his body. They always woke him early in the morning. Usually he kept his eyes closed, enjoying the luxurious warmth to which he was unaccustomed in the city. This morning he kept them closed for a different reason.

He felt as if his body had been turned inside out and his brain were grasped in a hot, sweating hand.

During the night, he vaguely recalled, he had been half awakened by some curious, fear-fraught twisting of the entire universe, it seemed. Everything had turned upside down and inside out. He had found himself shivering on the cold floor. Dizzy, weak, he clambered back into bed and fell into a tortured sleep.

Now he opened his eyes, afraid of what he might see.

He screamed hoarsely and hopped off the bed. His eyes burned in their sockets, transmitting to his brain pictures that he knew could never be. Though his mind remained cool, telling the rest of him that it was only a touch of sunstroke, he rushed madly, clothed in his sweat-soaked pajamas, through the house.

"Harry!" he shrieked. "Harry! I've gone insane!"

When he dashed, stumbling, into the bedroom, Worthing was sitting on the edge of his bed, staring around him fearfully.

Lanse rushed up to him seizing his shoulders. "I've gone mad!" he shouted harshly. "I can see right through you. I can see right through the walls of the house!"

He could see every vein, every artery, every muscle and organ in Worthing's body. When he looked around, he could see empty rooms, Worthing's wife and mother sitting up in bed dazedly, the servants downstairs, on the ground floor, preparing breakfast though they trembled and shook with fear. He could see outside the house, and what he saw there filled him with despair for his sanity.

Worthing sighed, apparently with relief. "I thought I was the only one," he said. "But you can see through everything, too, and so can I. So it's not so bad."

"You can, too?" Lanse exploded. "Good! Then it's a normal condition—temporarily, at least."

He immediately let go of Worthing's shoulder and rushed down the stairs and out into the wide grounds. Astounded, he stopped. Nothing here to convince him of his sanity. Worse —what he saw made him more sure he was mad.

In the mornings he was accustomed to come out on the great stretch of green lawn after breakfast to enjoy the mild warmth. The house was on top of a low hill, with tall woods starting a hundred yards from the base of the little plateau. A drive climbed the slow incline, leading through the bright lawn to the front of the house and around to the garages in the back.

Now he could see the small lake in the middle of the woods, though the trees surrounded it in a thick cluster.

Conical wigwams were gathered around the hill, with trees growing up through them. Indians—he was amazed that he could see so distinctly without his glasses—stood numbly in small groups around their camp.

He was startled by a series of crashes; when he searched for their cause, he discovered that the wind caused trees, supported by other trees, to fall to the ground. There were millions of trees, one growing within and around the other, uprooting some, a number hanging suspended on the branches of usurpers.

The Sun was not darkened, and yet something stood between the house and its rays.

Surrounding it and rearing a thousand feet up into the air, and extending a quarter of a mile in each direction of its base, a gargantuan building inclosed house and trees as completely as if the entire location and all it contained were playthings in a nursery.

He looked up. On the floors, diminishing far into the heavens, he could see thousands of people staring down at him and the crazy surroundings.

Through the walls he saw a vast airship floating aimlessly about, evidently as much surprised as any one on the ground. It hovered, seeking a familiar secureness.

Everything was transparent to his all-perceiving eyes. He was even able to trace the colossal foundations of the building that towered a quarter of a mile above him.

The Indians came out of their stupor first. Wildly brandishing their spears and bows, they came tilting at him. He laughed, for the walls of the giant structure were between them. But they tore through them as easily as if steel and concrete were air.

Then he shrieked insanely and dashed for the doubtful security of the house.

III.

LAWRENCE GREY wanted to kick himself. The captain promised himself that luxury as soon as he could leave the cramped cabin of his large amphibian with safety. There was something funny about it, too, he had to admit to himself, for the day before he had been consumed with a patriotic fire, when the desire to do something heroic for his country.

It had seemed like a brave, patriotic gesture to leave for a nonstop flight to Africa on July 4th. Now he felt like a fool, risking his life senselessly, with no particularly good chance of his landing in one piece at Zanzibar, a distance of twenty-five thousand miles from San Francisco, his starting point; and it made no difference whether he succeeded or failed.

He glanced rapidly at his oil and gasoline gauges, altimeter and radio compass. Then he began to make a few quick additions in his mind that aroused a raging fear.

He was able to make a speed of three hundred and ten miles an hour cruising. The entire trip would take approximately four days, with six or seven hours' sleep any time he wanted it every twenty-four hours, since the robot pilot would keep the ship flying in a straight line at a certain height.

But he carried scarcely enough gas and oil to make the hop. If he ran into a slight breeze head-on, he'd probably have to land quite a stretch away from Zanzibar.

Nice boys financing the trip! He'd be damned if he'd take any wild chances like that. He could make Singapore easily, without taking any long chances. Have to pass over it, anyhow.

That's what he'd do, he determined.

So he edged two points to the north. Instead of bringing him over New Guinea and the Dutch East Indies, as his old route would have done, he now headed for Micronesia, the archipelago between Guam and New Guinea. He was making excellent time. At twenty-nine minutes after one that afternoon he had passed the one hundred and eightieth meridian, and instead of traveling into the late afternoon of July 5th, it was the 6th. Now it was twenty-three minutes to six, and he was flying over the Caroline Islands.

The decision he had made lightened his spirits considerably. He permitted himself to whistle a tuneless song. By this time the next day he'd be in Singapore, taking it easy. And he wanted to know what Singapore, the hell hole of the world, was like.

Something seemed queer to him as he took his eyes off the gauges and peered toward the water. It was darkening rapidly now, though the sky was clear. And despite the fact that the only wind blowing was the wash of the propeller, the sea was rough and choppy, raising tall, white-topped waves.

He flew as low as he dared, skimming at low speed a hundred feet from the threshing water. A thrown lever lowered the left window.

Suddenly he heard, above the roar of tumultuous waves, screams of thousands of people. He shook his head impatiently, thinking the long stretch at the controls had made him feverish.

No! A moment more found him over an area of tortured water that was black with bobbing heads. Incoherent, meaningless shrieks of horror reached his ears. A few faces turned whitely up to him. As he stared in numb awe, hundreds went down, leaving only bubbles to be thrown about by the violent whitecaps.

He shot the nose upward for eight hundred feet elevation and searched the surface desperately. A vast area was visible to him, and the entire circle of vision was covered with bobbing heads, millions of them.

With nerveless fingers he threw the switch of the radio. Then he called, shakily, for his San Francisco headquarters. A moment later a voice weakly told him to go ahead.

"Captain Grey speaking," he said. "I'm over the Caroline Islands, longitude 158°23'west, latitude 8°30'north. There're millions of people drowning all around me. What shall I do?"

Immediately a mess of foreign polyglot jammed his radio. He listened dazedly to the incomprehensible roar of combined tongues for a long while, then gazed unnerved at the helpless millions of doomed people he could not aid.

IV.

THE INDIANS were at the foot of the hill, swiftly mounting the gentle slope. Lanse turned and ran for the house, yelling for help, his heart pounding wildly. Yet he felt apart, detached from the reality of the nightmare event. It was too mad to be actual.

But he ran, nevertheless. As his short legs pumped ambitiously, he kept turning his head to look over his shoulder at the Indians, who were rapidly shortening the distance between them. He knew he reached the door and put out his hand to turn the knob.

He felt nothing where the door should have been. At first he thought he had not quite reached the door and pushed on a few paces farther, only to find himself within the house, the door shut tightly, and the Indians still charging. He had walked through the door, apparently. There was no other way he could have come into the house without opening the door. But he refused to believe it.

He stood still, breathing hard from exertion. The Indians still rushed on. Let them rush! He couldn't move another step.

Suddenly three men strode purposefully through the opposite wall of the house. It was faintly comical to him—the determination with which they marched through that wall. In their hands were things that looked comfortingly like revolvers.

Without glancing at him they walked to the door, threw it open and faced the Indians. In a single gesture, they raised their arms all at once and tiny puffs emitted from the guns. Lanse wanted to fall to the floor and cry, perhaps; he wanted to do something that would express the childishness of such play. Like strong Napoleons, the three had marched through the walls to fire popguns at Indians.

He was amazed to see the red men stop short, their facial muscles taut as whipcord, the tensed body muscles standing out in great bunches. Their eyes held the brimming horror of men who stared at the gaunt face of death.

And then they toppled over and rolled down the incline of the hill.

The three came back into the room. Lanse wanted to thank them. Their stern, set faces forbade it. He let them speak first.

"What are you doing here?" the eldest asked.

Lanse was stunned. "The same thing you are, probably," he replied.

"And what is that?" one wanted to know.

"Living here," he answered.

"Do you know what date this is?" the eldest asked again.

Lanse shrugged, "In my time it was June 5, 1942. The only thing that's certain is that it is summer; the year depends on —well, it depends on what year you were living in when all this happened."

"When what happened?" the eldest demanded.

"When time went off half cocked."

They looked at each other. "I do not understand," the youngest said. "If it relates to the fourth dimension, we cannot comprehend. We are only mechanics of the machines."

"You may speak to our experts on the subject," the eldest offered. "There are several in this building."

Just then Worthing entered the room. He looked from one to the other, astounded.

"Is this your friend?" one asked Lanse.

Lanse nodded.

"Then both of you may come. Is he also an Einsteinian expert?"

"No," Lanse answered. "He is merely a rich man."

They did not understand the term.

"He is a rich man," Lanse explained, "because other men work for him."

"You mean they do the work he should rightfully do?"

"Not necessarily. He pays them for it."

"Pays them?" one echoed. "With what?"

It was getting too involved. Lanse hardly cared to explain the economic theory of his time. He changed subject by asking how their guns worked.

They looked down at the small machines as if for the first time.

"There are nicotine-filled capsules in them," the youngest said. "The capsules are contained in tiny steel needles that force the extremely soluble capsules into the blood stream. The nicotine is immediately carried to the heart and lungs and kills by arresting respiration and circulation in approximately one second."

Worthing liked the idea. It was immeasurably superior to the crude firearms he knew. With revolvers, the purpose was simply to tear a large hole in the body, trusting to chance to kill immediately by hitting a vital organ, or else causing death by excessive loss of blood. This was genteel, humane, slaughter.

While walking through the endless corridors toward the lifts, Lanse examined their new friends. At least he hoped they were friends. They were blond, tall, and powerful. The three were dressed exactly alike—green silklike shorts, green jerseys that left the arms and most of the muscular shoulders bare, brief green socks, and sandals.

"Are all the men blond?" Lanse asked.

They stared at him in amazement. "Of course. We're Nordic, aren't we?"

"Apparently."

They passed a number of the tall, blond inhabitants of the giant structure, mostly men, but several women also, and they were quite as tall as the men, though proportionately less powerfully built. All who passed examined the shorter twentieth-century men curiously, suspicious of something that Worthing and Lanse could not understand.

"We're not exactly welcome here, are we?" Lanse asked.

The tall, young mechanic looked down at him. "You shall find out later," he replied, in a tone that meant everything and nothing.

V.

A PARTY of twelve was fishing off Montauk Point, on Long Island, for tuna and swordfish. It was in the early morning of July 5th; the Sun had scarcely risen above the horizon; it was cool, the water motionless and warm. All twelve had enjoyed an excellent night's sleep, despite the momentary vertigo they found they had all suffered during the night, probably due to the inferior quality of imported Scotch they had enjoyed the evening before.

The host, Dr. Albert Crawford, was inclined to argue on that point, but since he had become sick also, he could only swear at the fact that America was the dumping ground of cheap alcohols.

Everything was all right now, though. They had slept well in spite of that and expected a great haul.

Captain Creary and his assistant, "Hard-tack" McNutt, cast the small converted coastguard runner loose and headed out three miles to sea. Meanwhile the twelve men, free from marital and financial worries, set about raising their jubilant spirits to Olympian heights.

By the time Captain Creary had sighted a large school of half-grown herring breaking water—which meant large fish of unknown species—they were in a magnificent state of artificial joy. Two of them were sitting in the baskets of chum, the ground bait that would be cast overboard to attract fish of all sorts, disgusted with the unaccustomed moisture. The others were lolling or flopping about on the smooth deck, laughing at the funny spectacle.

"Here we are, gentlemen," Captain Creary called out when he had cut around the furiously jumping school of silvery bright herring and now idled with the stern to the flashing excitement.

Hard-tack pulled the two out of the baskets and heaved the white mass overboard. No sooner had he done that than the frightened young herrings turned toward the boat, forgetful of their fear.

The sportsmen staggered to their feet and prepared their rig for heavy battle. As they lined up to the rail there was no evidence of intoxication other than their staggering; years of practice had trained their arms and eyes into extraordinary coördination, for they placed every cast precisely where they wanted it.

For half an hour they fished, without result. They followed that scintillating school of fear-stricken herring, casting exactly at the most moiled part of the school, where the disturbance was, but without a taker.

At last a lawyer named Sowers grew impatient. "What's the largest thing you've got in the ice box?" he asked.

Captain Creary debated a moment. "A big leg of mutton," he replied. "But it's too smackin' big fer any damned fish in these waters."

"The hell with that!" Sowers snapped. "Haul it out."

Hard-tack protested that it had already been cooked, was to make their main meal, and quoted the high price he had paid for it. Sowers was stonily insistent.

Captain Creary had to haul the leg of mutton out of the ice box. He watched despairingly as Sowers fumblingly skewered it on his great steel hook and heaved it over the side as far as he could cast it.

No sooner had it hit the water in the center of disturbance than an enormous black head reared and seized it before it could sink more than a few inches. Two small eyes at the sides of the slimy, black leather head, long ivory teeth that flashed in the sunlight—that was all they could see before it had swum out of sight, bent on more food.

Sowers excitedly snapped back his strong pole, sinking the hook deep into the mouth. A second later a violent yank on his reel hauled yards of steel line into the blue water. He let it run a hundred yards or so before he set the slow drag.

Immediately he had done so the others were horrified to see him fly over the railing and hit the water with a sharp splash. He still held the rod in his hand, treading water dazedly the while.

The school of herring circled away swiftly, leaving him alone by the side of the boat. For a moment he was pulled out to sea; then, the express-train speed ceased, and he drifted slowly, still holding the rod.

"Drop it!" they shouted.

Dr. Crawford threw him a lifebelt and line. Sowers grabbed at it, white with fear.

No man could speak or shout in the seconds that followed. All were stricken dumb with terror.

A black, barrel-shaped body, twenty feet long and a neck the same length, crowded down on poor Sowers, who could only gape at it.

Crawford gained his voice first. "Ichthyosaurus!" he screamed. "Swim! It eats only fish."

But one could scarcely expect the minute reptilian brain of the alien ichthyosaurus to realize that fact. It took precisely two seconds for it to cut Sowers to pieces and swallow the gory result. Then it turned its attention to the boat, capsizing it and eating all but Hard-tack McNutt. Its stomach capacity must have been enormous.

Hard-tack was later picked up by a strange airship as he clung to the pitiful wreckage. The weird airship, in combination with the horripilous events, rendered him completely insane.

VI.

THE ROOM into which Lanse and Worthing were ushered was fairly large. Their three guides were extremely respectful to the four men seated at separate desks; after bowing quite low, they left silently.

"You are of the nineteenth or twentieth century, are you not?" one asked, examining their clothing carefully.

"Twentieth," Lanse replied.

He looked around the room, trying to read some of the titles of the thousands of books lining the walls, but the distance was too great, and, besides, the books had an uncomfortable habit of seeming to turn inside out so that he could see the individual pages. It was as though he was looking at the magic blocks, watching them shift from visible bases to tops.

"Are you fourth-dimensional experts?"

"Well, you could call me that. My friend is just a rich man."

As soon as they heard that, they became more cordial and gave the two of them chairs to pull up to the desks. Lanse and the four others broke into a rapid fire of incomprehensible talk, of which Worthing could understand only occasional words —finite closed space in infinite space, dimensional extension, hyper-time, and not many more.

For hours they talked, Worthing growing more and more bored. At last Lanse turned to him.

"I feel like a child in comparison with these men," he said. "There were hundreds of phenomena we couldn't understand that're prefectly clear now."

"But you must remember," said one smilingly, "we built on

your foundations. The amount of work you did with such limited conditions is positively amazing.''

Lanse reddened with pleasure. It was the first bit of praise he had ever had from any one he respected. Like wine it quickened his blood, and he became confused, where before his explanations were clear-cut and concise as a written treatise.

"We've been trying to discover what's happened to the universe," he explained to Worthing. "These four men, Kant, Bassington, Reede, and Russo, are among the most eminent Einsteinian experts of the twenty-sixth century. They've collected a lot of data that we could hardly understand with our present knowledge——"

"In fact," Russo interrupted, "it's probable that we'll never succeed in understanding the results of this cataclysm. Or at best, the slightest amount of study and research will overthrow our most ironclad laws."

Lanse nodded agreement.

"I think that's not quite right," Reede contradicted. "In all likelihood we shall discover that the same laws, with many extensions, will apply to our changed environment."

Kant and Bassington shrugged.

"We know so little of our new conditions, it's better to avoid all prior theorizing," Kant said.

"What the deuce has happened?" Worthing demanded, baffled.

Lanse twisted his chair around to face him. I'll try to make it as simple as I can, though you won't understand quite a lot of it, because we don't either. And I suppose I'll have to avoid raising any two-sided points; it's hard enough without having to make corrections.

"To start from the beginning: Our universe can be compared to a gas, which is only an analogy and not to be taken as fact.

The reason we can compare the structure of the universe to that of a gas is because of the tremendous spaces between the molecules, or solar systems. However, that's as far as we dare bring the analogy. So far as we know, the molecule is the smallest particle of matter that retains the property of the whole. If that is correct, then our universe, which consists of ninety-two elements and their compounds, does not comply with that definition.

"It is only because the submicroscopic molecule and our cosmic molecule obey practically the same physical laws that I bother to remind you of this theory; more to the point—the accident that occurred so recently is happening a billion times a second in the atomic world.

"In the Brownian movement of molecules, we can see these particles rush toward each other, seem to crash, then fly from each other at furious speed. The paths they had followed are changed, and the loss of energy is so small that we can say these mutual repulsions are effected without loss of energy, because of the perfect elasticity of the bodies. We cannot determine the physical result on the two molecules, but we do know they are not destroyed.

"That is as far as the likeness goes.

"What happened to our universe was this: A fourth-dimensional star approached our solar system in the wrong direction, traveling at such a terrific speed that our eighteen miles per second was rendered negligible by comparison; in other words, where the comparison of speeds or energy renders one speed or energy so infinitely small that it has no effect on the result, we ignore the speed or energy.

"Thus we say our solar system, in relation to the fourth-dimension star, was fixed in space. The other star, moving at nearly the speed of light, consequently with infinite mass, did not actually strike the Sun, but it warped the hyper-space separating the two systems so effectively that its infinite speed was transmitted without loss to our solar systems.

"Just how that was done is not particularly difficult to understand. Gravity, Einstein says, is due to the warping of space; therefore the warping of the interstellar hyper-space was comparable for a brief moment to the bending of a cosmic catapult that hurled our solar system from the fourth-dimensional star at the rate of speed at which the interloper approached—nearly the speed of light. The probable result, since the transmission of energy and speed from the fourth-dimensional star to our Sun was brought about with practically no loss either of energy or speed, was that the invading star was repelled in the opposite direction, causing it to travel in the orbit of the solar system and at a speed of eighteen miles a second.

"In other words, the speed, energy, and dimensional attributes of the invader were given over to us; the energy and speed left over were passed on to the other star, so that it cannot travel at more than eighteen miles a second, nor have more than three dimensions.

"Besides the adoption of the infinite speed, mass, and energy, we have been the proud receivers of the burden of four dimensions."

"What!" Worthing gasped, turning from one to the other, dazed.

The scientists of the twenty-sixth century nodded.

"Certainly!" Kant said. "At a speed approximating that of light, a body possesses infinite mass, two dimensions are infinitely extended, length is contracted almost to infinity, and time exists at right angles to the three other dimensions."

"But why didn't the two stars collide?" Worthing asked.

"You can have the formula of molecular pressure in collisions, if you want to determine the pressure exerted between the stars,'' Kant offered. ''It won't do you much good, because you can't find the speed or mass of the other star. Why bother with that, though? We're spinning through space at one hundred and sixty-nine thousand miles a second, and I, of the twenty-sixth century, can talk to you, of the twentieth. We need no better proof.''

Worthing stared bewilderedly at Kant, who was frightened at seeing him topple off the chair in a faint.

''Believe me,'' Lanse said calmly as the others dashed about trying to revive the unconscious man, ''I feel like doing the same thing.''

To Be Continued

DENNIS HILDRETH, Son of Kildreth (sorry about that), sets us straight on a misread signature:

Upon looking at the recently published PR #97 I was both surprised and pleased to find out that you published my history of PR. However, after getting over my surprise, I was very displeased to find out that you spelled my name wrong!

As you know, a lot of fans are complaining that when the last PR rolls off the press, they will long since be dead. Well, I have an announcement to make. I have found a way to read all the PRs. What you do is go into suspended animation. Then, once a year, you come out S.A. and read up on last years PRs. Since this may take a week to do, that means that in 52 years, you would have only aged a year! Think of all the PRs you would be able to read!

R. DEAN RUTGERS, 769 E. Wiser Lake Rd., Lynden/WA 98264, thought #78 great.

First off, thanks for printing those German PR fan letters. It is now possible for all PR clubs in America to have a library of the latest original PR's by simply sending our copies over there in exchange for theirs.

Secondly, I have found the perfect solution to your problem with your artist Gray Morrow. Let's send Morrow to Germany to do their covers and hire Kelly Freas to replace him.

Thirdly, PR ranks easily with the great S!F! which came from the 40's and 50's which is why it is far superior to present day SF.

Fourthly, if PR #78 (Power Key) does not win the Hugo award, I for one will be deeply disappointed. I have yet to read a novel this year that even comes close to the quality of PR #78.

BANG! BANG!—you're dead, Future Slang . . . says GERALD L. TONNE, 112½ 5th St. NW, Waverly/IA 50677.

In issue #94 you asked for comments on your "future slang", so I decided to respond. Of everything included in *Perry Rhodan*, I find this invention of yours to be the most irritating. (I hate it with a passion.) Its insertion into the text seems out of place and artificial. Though I don't doubt your sincerity and good intentions in this venture, please desist! For that matter, why bother with slang at all? If you can edit in your singular words and phrases, it should certainly be no more difficult to remove any "right on!" or "hey, man!" you should stumble across. Most major science fiction writers do not depend upon slang, either present or future. This gives the story the ability to age gracefully. I urge you to reconsider your use of "future slang", and discontinue it.

It was most enjoyable to read PR #95 because the plot did not hinge on some million-to-one and rather unbelievable random happening. (For example, another intelligent species blundering upon Khrest's retirement planet almost before Rhodan had a chance to leave.) Too many of the current plots have taken this unlikely device for their basis. Of course there's nothing you can do about it, but one wonders how credulous the authors felt their readers were.

Thank you for your time and consideration.

RHOFANS who agree with our previous reader are advised not to read this letter as it makes liberal use of that Ackermonstrosity, Future Slanguage. It comes from the PUT Administrator, address at end of letter.

I love PR! I would certainly mourn his grot. PR books are a grass! I'm starting a subsidary of a PR club. It's called PUT, People for the Unification of Terra. I'm quite worried about mankind's destruction, just as Perry was. Although I don't have the technology of the Arkonides to help me, I'm depending on logic. I believe I'm absolutely right when I say "United We Survive. Divided We Perish!" Don't think PR influenced me although it helped. I've only been reading PR for the past year and I bought 62 books in that time. If your wondering, I'm not spaggy! I've already written to some fan club presidents and to the President! If any of you have the same feelings I do or want more info write to— PUT - Administrator, 4B S. Dooley Ave., Richmond, VA 23221. Send an SASE along, please. I mean it when I say this could be "The Late Great Planet Earth" unless we take action. Forvala phod trex, epon?

AN AWFUL LOT of questions are asked by GEOFFREY TOLLE of 1911 Fairview Pl., Alliance/OH 44601. In order to answer them all intelligently we might possibly have to read thru more than 600 future German PRs, whereas we are at the presentime only about 15 stories ahead of the rest of you in translating.

As I read some of the latest issues of PR I became aware that they have become increasingly more interesting. I believe the Akons are by far the best feature so far. In fact I foresee the upcoming battle between Akon and Terra as one of prime importance and one decided through Auris and Perry.

Now I have a few things to say and ask 1) don't say that this is the last time the Perry poster will be available, you know, as well as I, that depends on reader demand (the President of Ace told me to my face: "5000—PERIOD." FJA); 2) when do we see the MS again; 3) did Rhodan ever revisit the robot hall on Vagabond; 4) when will Rhodan revisit the planet Isan (Issue 45); 5) how did the Volation queen determine that Sikeron was immune to aging (47); 6) wasn't Perry able to use the teleportation devices in the singers (36); 7) when does Perry start to use the infra-red Laser; 8) when does he revisit the Living Planet (issue 93); 9) did Perry take the Molecular Deformers ship apart to see what technical equipment he could find?

A SATISFIED SUBSCRIBER SAYS:

Dear Kris,

I just thought I'd drop a short line to you to say "THANKS" for handling the Perry Rhodan series and making it available to those people who couldn't get it otherwise. Especially for someone like me! And though I have a "STARS & STRIPES BOOK STORE" on POST—to count on it for my PR's is nearly impossible. And I'm truly glad for the service you provide!

And to humanize the several subscriptions I've had with you and to give you a background on one of your subscribers —STANLEY E. SCHRIEFFER is 29 years of age, at present a tanker stationed in Germany. Before I joined the Army in 1974, I was a professional Mechanical Draftsman with a 2 year Associate Degree in the LIBERAL ARTS & SCIENCE—majored in history, sociology and computers. And my main lifetime ambition is to be a science fiction ADVENTURE writer. My hobbies are WRITING, READING PR and playing HISTORICAL WARGAMES.

I discovered PR in January 1974 when I was looking for some good adventurous SCI-FI to read in my spare time. I began with #38 & 39. And halfway thru #38 I found I had to read the entire story-line. Today I have 1 to 93 in English and I have about 43 of the series in its original language of German. I also have the year book in German. And I love the series! It's the best series to hit the science fiction shelves.

I used to be an ardent fan of Robert Heinlein. But when I ran across the PR series—the things which R.A.H. dreamed about, PR was putting into practice. And where R.A.H. speculates —PR turns it into an "imaginary reality." And *also* where R.A.H. makes the reader feel like MAN leaves a lot to be desired—PR gives MAN hope, promise and a future. And where R.A.H.'s are short books of short duration, PR's infinite number makes it all seem a SPACE OPERA of a more personal touch with the reader, and gives the reader something to look forward to with hope and promise—even if it is another PR itself!

All in all—the Perry Rhodan series can teach a lot of American Science fiction writers a thing or two! Especially about getting all the different SCI-FI Concepts into a workable story-line and stop being so fragmented by having to go to different writers for different subjects like ESP in the future to man's conquest of space. PR has it ALL TOGETHER!! And I feel that's another reason why PR is GREAT. PR can teach science fiction through adventure!

BILL COX grumps from Lawrenceville/GA:

It is bad enough that the covers on PR don't fit, but now the blurps on the back cover are lies as well. Who writes that trash any way? Surely it can't be Forry. *(Guilty.)* The description of the monsters on the back of #94 was ridiculous, as was the cover. You should fire Gray Morrow if he can't illustrate the stories more accurately. *(Like Wilson's work any better?)* *Horn: Green* was even worse. The cover I mean. Also the back; John Pincer didn't have a thing to do with the Akons. As for the PRs themselves, they were good, even though in one Perry was made to look like an idiot (#97). I disliked ARLEEN very much. If that was the result of the editor's coup I'd hate to see him pick a bad story. I also hate THE PR MAN; Tim Whalen and his stupid Rhocom. It is plain to see that the juvenile section is making a cult of PR the way they did STAR TREK. Such fanaticism disgusts me. More FIAWOL!!! Yuch!!!

DAVID M. LUND of 5807 W. Rois Rd., Richmond/VA 23227 has applause for "Mr. Jaws"

I thoroughly enjoy the PERRY RHODAN series. Although I only have 39 at the moment, I soon plan to subscribe. I am looking forward to adventure 100, "Desert of Death".

Now for the stories. I didn't think I'd enjoy ACTION: DIVISION 3 but I did! That plot to rescue the crew of life-boat

Carolina 2 was brilliant, and disguising the vessel as the local version of Mr. Jaws, the Lidiok, really had me fooled! The only complaint is that those Springers are getting to my nerves. And I do hope you'll have more of that old farmer, Ez Rhyker. He was great!

As for THE PLASMA MONSTER, that was quite exciting. The Akons, those pre-Arkonides, figured, as well as the Aras. In this one, Rhodan took great pains to admit he wasn't a dictator. Of course he . . . Well, anyway, it was rather gruesome. Plasma taking over the world, death everywhere . . . how do we get into all these messes?

Now for the departments: the Editorial was great. Especially in PLASMA MONSTER, by our fair translator Wendy Ackerman. It listed the addresses of some German fans. Also, the serial, "The Sunken World", is one of the best ones you've had. Of course it's not true (ask Atlan—he'll tell you Atlantis was an Arkonide colony) but it's great anyhow.

Your new feature, the PR Man, is excellent. Tim Whalen is very informative. However, the new mini-serial, "Arleen", is not very good. The shock-short, "Alien Tongue", was exactly what a shocking shock-short should be. Likewise, "The Atlantean Chronicles", was very good.

PERENNIAL PERRYSCOPER HENRY DAVIS JR. of Baker Station Rd., Goodlettsville/TN lets us know his interesting opinions as usual.

Blazing Sun (strangely named) provided modest reading. The 110,000 Arkonides might end up to be more of a hinderance than a help to Atlan, if Ceshal decides that he possesses the bearing of a regal Arkonide and that Atlan lacks these qualities.

Rocklynne's "The Diversifal" was a good enough story of

the typical time paradox. Not as good as "Quietus" but satisfying. It reminds me of another SF story I once read. Only the guy was hung on something about "I'll be a pie-eyed emu" or something. Maybe you remember it.

I've never read *Star-Begotten*. But it seems very much like a novel I just finished, John Taine's *Seeds of Life*. Only this time it is an artificially evolutionized human who wants to elevate mankind. Rather than elevate, he almost retrogresses the human race. Rather gruesome at the end.

Cummings' "The Man of the Meteor" is finally drawing to a close. Perhaps I should be thankful because it does drag a little. Hopefully the final battle scene will make your revival of this story worthwhile.

The Atlantean Chronicles (Chapter 6) provided an entertaining discussion. I disagree with Hoerbiger's hypothesis. He seems to take it for granted that large planetoids drift through the Solsystem and come near to earth. That depends too much on chance to be true. Wagner's concept is also hard to swallow. I do believe that at one time all the continents were a single land mass and gradually drift apart.

#87 (The Starless Realm) by Darlton: Apparently It has recovered (slightly) from the effects of Semispace. Certainly enough to send Perry, Sengu, and Pucky to find out the plight of Barkon.

The plight of Barkon itself was not that interesting. What comes to light is the existence of the Invisibles—and It's relationship to them. My guess is that perhaps the Invisibles invaded Pel at one time and used the inhabitants (back when they were of flesh and blood) in some sort of bizarre experiment. Perhaps the Invisibles wanted to free their souls from their bodies and used them for it. Very much like the Skylark series. And perhaps the creature they created (IT) rebelled and expelled them out of the galaxy. Perhaps. But we'll see the Invisibles again. After all PR #118 is Attack of the Shadows and PR #133 is Station of the Invisibles. So . . .

Who is the Anti? He called Perry a barbarian? Another Arkonide?

Wilson's "Love" dwells a lot on the emotional aspects of a highly unusual love affair. While well written it offers only a temporary diversion from the more rowdy forms of SF which I prefer.

Thora Remembered is a beautiful poem. A fitting requiem for Thora. Sigh! And Mory-Abrolies so far in the future!

I couldn't help but notice Wenday's advertisement. How about serializing Tarrano the Conqueror? Cummings' excellent novel is too expensive to purchase.

"AND THE FIRST shall be last." Practically. GERALD L. TONNE, who appeared early in this issue's *Perryscope*, is heard from again with the penultimate letter.

Since the cut-off date for your survey has passed, I thought I would express my opinions on your series in the form of his letter. All criticisms are intended to be constructive, and I hope you will accept them as such. Should you feel any of my ideas worthy of consideration, I would appreciate your passing them on to the proper authority.

I am 22 years old and a college senior majoring in mathematics and chemistry. I will soon be working on a masters degree in computer science. I have been reading and collecting S.F. for 12 years. (My library contains about 400 volumes.) I have been with *Perry Rhodan* from the beginning, and own all the American volumes. I find *Perry Rhodan* an entertaining and decently written work, though placing it in the same class as Heinlein, Clarke, etc., (as some of your readers would,) is asking a bit much. The characters are too brittle, one dimensional, and stereotyped; while the plots are too often decided by "chance meetings." (One seemingly cannot travel 10 light years in a straight line without stumbling over some intelligent life form or other.) But all in all there is a definite place for this type of literature and I thoroughly enjoy it.

My main objection is to the cost and content of the magazine. I realize the cost of production is high, and being a firm believer in capitalism, you are surely entitled to a fair profit. So the actual cost per book cannot go down. But the truth of the matter is that P.R. is hardly worth the price paid. 100 to 110 pages of Rhodan does not match up to $1.25 plus tax. Every time I think that these 90 odd volumes could be novels by Poul Anderson or A.E. Van Vogt or Ray Bradbury or . . . , I want to cry. Though the short stories and serials are interesting enough, the book *does* exist for P.R. I would suggest that you drop all features except the Perryscope, and publish this plus *two* episodes of P.R. per volume. In this way you could convert a book of questionable value into a bargin without appreciably increasing the book size. (I buy the book for P.R., *not* the short stories etc.)

The only thing I really dislike about your magazine is the interjection of "future slang" into the text. I feel this only serves to detract from the material, and is disgusting in general. Please, spare us!

I would love to see P.R. expanded to four per month, but again would encourage you to give us more Rhodan and less filler.

Thank you for reading my ideas. I hope this input is in some way helpful. Enclosed is $1.00 for the Ackermuseum. Not much, but I hope it helps. Thank you.

(Thank you for your opinions and the donation. Every single dollar helps. A gift of just one dollar from every Rhodan reader would take the Fantasy Foundation—"Ackermuseum"—out of the red. But, alas, past responses suggest it will never happen in a million years . . . and by then I'll be 1,000,060 years old—if my cell showers are regularly renewed.)

DISCONTENT *was the theme of a* long *letter from* MIKE BUNCH, 808 S. Main St., Fairmount/IN 46928, *who emphasized that he is a true blue Rhofan and will always continue to read the magabook but is convinced that I am the wrong editor for PR, that I wouldn't even read his letter to begin with, and if I did I wouldn't publish it, and if I published it I wouldn't do anything about it. He was wrong on count 1—I read his letter as I do all letters to PR. He was right on count 2—I am not publishing all his complaints, rather I am summarizing the principal ones: that I have announced the separate bookazine* ATLAN, *the Missing Trio of PRs as a boxed set, the SPACE-SHIPS OF RHODANIA, the Free Poster that he hasn't received yet (at the time of my writing these words, which by the time they see print was 'way last June). Basically he doesn't believe that I give a damn what the readers want but go dictatorially on my own smug way. (Question: how long has it been since you've seen a* Scientifilm World? *Have you noticed any book-length serial lately? Have you antifuslangers been gratified to observe that the futuristic slang is thinning out? The point is, those things I* can *do something about, I do. YOU or YOU or YOU—or Mike Bunch, if he were to become Editor of PERRY RHODAN tomorrow—wouldn't have the power to force the publishers to publish ATLAN till they thought the time was ripe. Or issue the boxed books. Or anything else. They* thought *the*

183

time was ripe and Wendayne & I & Sig Wahrman & Stu Byrne did a great deal of work, preparing all the aforementioned works which so many of you have been waiting impatiently to purchase—then the publishers decided the time was not propitious after all. The publishers, not the editor. The power is with the publishers, not with editors. Publishers hire & fire editors, editors do not hire & fire publishers. Editors are more responsible to a publishers' Profit & Loss records than they are to readers' wants. Does ANYONE in their right mind, to hypothesize an extreme example to make the point CRYSTAL clear; does any reader really believe that if a vocal group of fans "demanded" PERRY RHODAN every day, with Frazetta covers, colored illustrations on the inside, serialization of the new works by Heinlein, Asimov, van Vogt & Clarke, a cover price of 50¢ and a free poster of Thora with every subscription; does ANYONE reading these words imagine for a moment that even if Andre Norton or L. Sprague de Camp were editor of PERRY RHODAN, they could give the readers what I can not?) Finally, riled reader Bunch thought I had a whole bunch of chutzpah—gall—nerve to ask readers for a dollar donation for my Museum of Imaginative Literature . . . and then be offended when they failed to respond in droves. Did it ever occur to me, he asked, that they might have more important things to spend their dollar on, such as gas or food or, as in his case, comicbooks for his own collection? In effect he says, Ackerman, you take care of your collection and I'll take care of mine. He received a long personal letter from me in response but whether "sweet reason" will reach him or not I have not found out yet. Stay tuned to this wavelength and perhaps in #108 we'll all find out. In the meantime, I seem rather to have written an Extemporaneous Editorial!

180° DIFFERENT in opinion from the foregoing Mike Bunch is **MARTY L. LEVINE** of 1023 Elizabeth St., Pittsburgh/PA 15221, who says succinctly:

I've never seen any professional editor as receptive to your readers as you are.

And in conclusion, a most warm & welcome, unexpected & appreciated, altruistic & amazing communique from ROGER ADAY, the Western Representative of the INTERNATIONAL FAN CLUB OF PERRY RHODAN SERIES (IFC), 913 N. Poplar, Wellington/KS 67152. The following message (in clear code) was received on a rare day when I, FJA, was ill in bed with some mysterious 48-hour 102°-temperature malady, the club's kind concern really made my day . . . also my week. Said Aday:

Dear Forry:

We at the IFC want to speak to all the other PR clubs in the US and other countries.

Enclosed is a check for $50.00, to be used for the Ackermansion. This is being contributed to you from all of us who are associated with the IFC.

Now, we offer a challenge to all of the other PR Clubs that receive the US editions of Perry Rhodan. We challenge you to match or beat our contribution. I'm sure that if you talk to your members, they will be glad to help. After all, they are members because of their great love for Perry Rhodan, and PR was brought to them through the unceasing efforts of Forry. Now we can do something BIG to thank him for bringing us PR. We can keep his life long dream alive by sending money!

MATCH US!!!! BEAT US!!! IF YOU BEAT US, WE'LL DO EVERYTHING IN OUR POWER TO EITHER MATCH OR BEAT YOUR HIGHER CONTRIBUTION!!! COME ON! WOULDN'T YOU LIKE TO SEE US HAVE TO DIG DEEPER AND BRING FORTH AN EVEN LARGER NUMBER? YOU CAN MAKE US DO IT BY BEATING OUR FIFTY DOLLARS! LET'S HEAR FROM YOU!!!!!!!!!!!!!!!!!!

PS: I sure hope this plan of ours works because we really want to see the Ackermansion turn into the Great Museum that it can if it is allowed to survive!!!

The letter was also signed STEVE WALTMAN, Eastern representative of the IFC. Forvala, karani! Shahntel, tanfondu. (Thanks a million!)

```
FJA: THE PERRYSCOPE
2495 Glendower Ave.
Hollywood/CA 90027
```

Canadians: Please send POSTAL MONEY ORDERS ONLY, payable in U.S. dollars.
PERRY RHODAN #108 thru . . . .

NAME (Print Clearly) ....

(AGE) ....

ADDRESS ....

CITY ....

STATE (Spell Out) ....

ZIP ....

COUNTRY ....

PERRY RHODAN SPACE CENTERS

ALABAMA

WATKINS BOOK SHOP
9168 Parkway East
Birmingham, Ala. 35206

PROFESSOR BOOK CENTER
2901 18th St. South
Homewood, Ala. 35209

CALIFORNIA

GARDEN GROVE BOOK SHOP
12926 Main St.
Garden Grove, Calif. 92640

READMORE
120 East Avenue J
Lancaster, Calif. 93534

THE GOLDEN QUESTION BOOKSHOP
2218 Mac Arthur Blvd.
Oakland, Calif. 94602

DISTRICT OF COLUMBIA

UNIVERSAL NEWSSTAND
735 14th St. N.W.
Washington, D.C.

FLORIDA

O'HENRY'S UNIVERSITY BOOKSTORE
5406 Stirling Rd.
Davie, Fla. 33314

KANSAS

RECTOR'S BOOK STORES INC.
206 East Douglas
Wichita, Kansas 67202

MASSACHUSETTS

SIGHT & SOUND, INC.
173 Cambridge St.
Boston, Mass. 02114

MASSACHUSETTS

THE SCIENCE FANTASY BOOKSTORE
18 Eliot Street
2nd Floor-Harvard Sq.
Cambridge, Mass. 02138

DUNHAM MALL BOOK SHOP
31 Dunham Mall
Pittsfield, Mass. 01201

MINNESOTA

PAGE ONE BOOKSHOP
712 Laurel St.
Brainerd, Minn. 56401

NEW JERSEY

FAIR HAVEN BOOK STORE
759 River Road
Fair Haven, N.J. 07701

GALLERY EAST BOOKSTORE
103 Third Ave.
Neptune City Shopping Center
Neptune City, N.J. 07753

PASSAIC BOOK CENTER
594 Main Avenue
Passaic, N.J. 07055

NEW YORK

COLLINS STATIONERY
124 West Post Road
White Plains, N.Y. 10606

NORTH CAROLINA

D.J.'s NEWSCENTER
North Hills Mall
Raleigh, N.C. 27612

D.J.'s COLLEGE BOOK & NEWS
2416 Hillsborough St.
Raleigh, N.C. 27607

D.J.'s NEWS & BOOK
Crabtree Valley Mall
Raleigh, N.C. 27612

OHIO

KAY'S BOOK & MAG. SUPERMARKET
620 Prospect Avenue
Cleveland, Ohio 44115

NEWS DEPOT
358 High St.
Hamilton, Ohio 45011

GOLDEN TRIANGLE BOOK STORE
516 S. Locust St. (Tollgate Mall)
Oxford, Ohio 45056

AMERICAN BOOK & NEWS
5781 Ridge Rd.
Parma, Ohio 44129

OKLAHOMA

RECTOR'S BOOK STORE INC.
4813 N. May Ave
Oklahoma City, Okla. 73112

OREGON

THE BOOK VAULT
3125 S.W. Cedar Hills Blvd.
Beaverton, Ore. 97005

THE BOOK VAULT
3rd & Main
Hillsboro, Ore. 97123

THE GALLERY BOOKSTORE
220 Liberty N.E.
Salem, Ore. 97301

THE LOOKING GLASS BOOKSTORE
421 S. W. Taylor St.
Portland, Ore. 97204

SOUTH DAKOTA

COVER TO COVER
Brookings Mall
Brookings, S. Dakota 57006

TEXAS

COCHRAN'S BOOKSTORE
4521 West Gate Blvd.
Austin, Texas 78745

TEXAS

UNIVERSITY CO-OP
2246 Guadalupe
Austin, Texas 78705

BOOKS N THINGS
314 Cove Terrace S/Ctr.
Copperas Cove, Texas 76522

THE BOOK STORE
9348 Dyer
El Paso, Texas 79924

THE BOOK STORE
6003 Mesa
El Paso, Tx. 79912

THE BOOK STORE
9518 Viscount
El Paso, Tx. 79925

ACE NEWS
8180 Main St.
Houston, Texas 77025

BELLAIRE NEWS
5807 Bellaire Blvd.
Houston, Texas 77036

BOOK DEN on RICE BLVD.
2510 Rice Blvd.
Houston, Texas 77005

GUYS NEWS
3622 Main St.
Houston, Texas 77002

ALAMO BOOK STORE #21
North Star Mall
San Antonio, Texas 78228

ALAMO BOOK STORE #11
214 Central Park Mall
San Antonio, Texas 78216

ALAMO BOOK STORE #10
175 Valley Hi Mall
San Antonio, Texas 78227

ALAMO BOOK STORE #14
McCreless Mall
San Antonio, Texas 78223

TEXAS

ALAMO BOOK STORE #8
Wonderland Mall
San Antonio, Texas 78201

ALAMO BOOK STORE #7
503 East Houston
San Antonio, Texas 78205

UTAH

BY'S MAGAZINE SHOP
Main Street
Salt Lake City, Utah 84119

WASHINGTON

GIBSON HOUSE, INC.
109 N. Tower
Centralia, Wash. 98531

WISCONSIN

BOOK WORLD
30 South Main
Janesville, Wisc. 53545

CANADA

BAKKA BOOKSTORE
282 to 286 Queen St. W.
Toronto, M5V 2A1
Ontario, Canada

PERRY RHODAN

Just $1.25 each

#61 **Death Waits in Semispace** Mahr

#62 **The Last Days of Atlantis** Scheer

#63 **The Tigris Leaps** Brand

#64 **Ambassadors from Aurigel** Mahr

#65 **Renegades of the Future** Mahr

#66 **The Horror** Voltz

#67 **Crimson Universe** Scheer

#68 **Under the Stars of Druufon** Darlton

#69 **The Bonds of Eternity** Darlton

#70 **Thora's Sacrifice** Brand

#71 **The Atom Hell of Grautier** Mahr

#72 **Caves of the Druufs** Mahr

#73 **Spaceship of Ancestors** Darlton

#74 **Checkmate: Universe** Mahr

#75 **Planet Topide, Please Reply** Brand

#76 **Recruits For Arkon** Darlton

#77 **Conflict Center: Naator** Darlton

#78 **Power Key** Scheer

#79 **The Sleepers** Voltz

#80 **The Columbus Affair** Scheer

Available wherever paperbacks are sold or use this coupon.